FOLLOW
THE
CRYPTO

STEPHEN W. KING

Lucas Bitterman series, Book Two

◆ FriesenPress

Suite 300 - 990 Fort St
Victoria, BC, V8V 3K2
Canada

www.friesenpress.com

This is a work of fiction. References to historical events, real people, or actual places are used fictionally, Other names, places, and event are the products of the author's imagination.

The poem Northwest Rivers by Eugene S. Fairbanks is used with permission of the poet.

ISBN
978-1-03-911623-8 (Hardcover)
978-1-03-911622-1 (Paperback)
978-1-03-911624-5 (eBook)

1. FICTION, MYSTERY & DETECTIVE, POLICE PROCEDURAL

Distributed to the trade by The Ingram Book Company

Dedicated to the memory of my brother, Rick.
He loved reading a good story. He also lived
and told more than a few great stories.

One

George Kennedy was startled awake by the sharp shake of his bed, his room, and the whole building. The following six seconds of rolling waves scared him. When the rolling stopped and he began to think clearly, he realized that he had experienced his first earthquake. He tentatively got out of bed and pulled on his jeans and the flannel shirt that had been lying on the floor where he had tossed it on his way to bed the previous night. Then, without bothering with socks, he slipped into his low-top hiking boots. He worried about his home business equipment and the integrity of the 1920s three-story brick structure in which his second-floor rented condo unit was located. George walked through his two-bedroom condo and turned on the lights. The power was good. A quick glance at his desk-top computer and printer confirmed they had power too. Nothing had fallen off the walls or shelves, as George had nothing on the walls and the shelves were empty. No furniture had upended, but he only had a bed and the two large folding tables on which his electronics sat. His cell phone had been knocked off its charger, but it appeared to be all that had been upset by the quake.

George picked up his phone, grabbed his coat, locked the two deadbolt locks on his unit, and went down the stairs to the street-level entrance. He wanted to see if the building had suffered any damage. The three-story brick structure had failing retail shops at street level, and someone had decided in the 1980s to convert the upper two floors into four condos to capitalize on the downtown condo-living boom at the time. The units did not sell and had been reimagined as rentals. George stood on the sidewalk and saw no apparent structural damage to the building. Maggie Schwartz, a middle-aged recent divorcee and the manager of a downtown clothing store who lived in 2B, walked up behind George.

"Well, that was some shake. Doesn't look there is any damage, though."

"Oh, hi, Maggie. You startled me. I guess I am a little jumpy. That was my first earthquake."

"I've had the privilege of surviving quite a few, but they do get your attention." She smiled mischievously and added, "You always remember your first. You see or hear either Auggie or the Larsons?"

George looked up toward the two units on the third floor and saw Harry Larson looking out the open window. "You okay, Harry?"

Susan Larson joined her husband at the window and shouted down, "Yeah, we're fine, but some of my Limoges statues fell off the shelf and broke."

George waved and hollered, "Glad you're okay. It doesn't look like there is any damage we can see down here. Have you seen Auggie?" Auggie Trimble, a retired fisherman and widower, was almost deaf and drank himself to sleep most nights. He lived right above George and seldom made a sound.

Harry hollered down, "I will check on him, but I bet he slept through the whole thing."

Maggie wrapped her terry robe tighter around herself and told George, "I'm cold and going to go back in. You coming?"

George looked at his watch, thought a second, and replied, "No, you go ahead. I am up and about, so I think I'll walk down to the Old Town Café and have breakfast. You take care, Maggie." He headed down Railroad Avenue, turned on Holly Street for the walk to his favorite breakfast haunt in Bellingham. Three blocks into his walk, George felt a shake from the sidewalk and naturally concluded, as if he had suddenly become an expert on earthquakes, that it was an aftershock.

When George walked into the restaurant, he was pleased that his usual table was vacant. No sooner had George sat down when Ellen brought a coffee pot and a cup and grinned. "That was some quake, huh, George?"

"Yeah, it knocked me and BOTH my girlfriends out of bed!"

"In your dreams, George. You want coffee?"

"Sure, and the usual, thanks."

As he waited for breakfast, George realized that he had been in Bellingham for almost two years, longer than he had ever landed anywhere and that maybe it was about time to move on. He certainly would not have trouble packing up his personal belongings; everything he owned would fit in the backseat and trunk of his cherished 2012 Mustang, except the bed and tables, which he planned on leaving behind. However, he needed another two or three weeks for his second business to play out. It was not immediately clear to George how he would be able to disentangle himself from his first job, short of simply walking away.

Ellen brought George his usual—a California omelet, bacon, and a side of potatoes. "How are the cards treating you, George?"

"Pretty good lately. I had a great day yesterday out at the Silver Reef. Maybe even enough to be able to leave a tip today, if I get some actual service." He smiled at Ellen, who knew that George always left a generous tip, unlike many of her regulars.

Two

Luke sat at the kitchen table, drinking coffee and reading the San Francisco Chronicle. The house was quiet; Annie and eight-month-old Ashley were still asleep. Contrary to his habits in college or law school, Lucas Bitterman woke early almost every day now, even on lazy Saturdays, like this day promised to be. His early rising began almost three years ago when he went through two schools that comprised boot camp for new agents in the Secret Service. Both the eleven-week course at the Federal Law Enforcement Training Center in Glynco, Georgia, and the seventeen-week course at the James J. Rowley Training Center in Washington, D.C., that followed it were grueling but exhilarating experiences.

When he came home for his first assignment in the San Francisco field office, the job had been demanding but also energizing—he loved the work. He awoke each morning looking forward to an interesting and demanding day. Then, to firmly imprint a new sleep schedule, Ashley was born. Luke put the paper down, took a sip of coffee, and thought, for the thousandth time this month, what a lucky guy he was: a wonderful wife, a beautiful baby girl, and an exciting job. It also helped that he had inherited their beautiful San Francisco Marina District home from his grandfather, just a couple of blocks from his mother's home.

The last three years had been eventful. Three years ago, he was a young man, confused about what he was going to do with his life. He had graduated from Berkeley with a degree in accounting, had passed the CPA exam, but found no joy or personal satisfaction in the work of accounting. He had then gone onto Hastings College of the Law and taken the bar exam twice. Then, while waiting for the results of the bar exam and after dealing with a problematic inheritance from his grandfather, a 1933 Double Eagle, he had learned of the Secret Service. He and Annie had decided that he should pursue the Secret Service as a career.

Luke looked around the kitchen and considered again the need to update and remodel the house. His grandfather had been totally engaged in his career as a physician and professor and had never shown much interest in the house, other than a place to sleep at night. However, his grandfather had been wise and knew that when Luke and Annie moved into the house, they would want to upgrade their new home, so he had included a substantial sum in Luke's inheritance specifically for a remodel. All Luke and Annie really needed to do was plan the project and get a contractor.

Luke's reverie was interrupted by a chimed notification from his cell phone, sitting on the charger on the kitchen counter. He grabbed his phone and saw his News Alert app had flashed a report:

> *Bellingham, WA. This morning at 6:36 PDT, a 6.0 magnitude earthquake hit Bellingham, Washington. Initial reports suggest no serious damage or injuries. The epicenter of the quake is tentatively located as twenty miles west of Bellingham and fifteen miles deep, in the Strait of Juan de Fuca. No tsunami alert has been issued.*

Luke closed the news app as Annie walked in the kitchen, wearing a robe, the silly kangaroo slippers Luke had gotten her for Christmas, and hair worthy of a wind tunnel. "Morning, hon, I'm glad to see you made a large pot of coffee. I'm going to need most of it. Ashley was up quite often last night, and I didn't get much sleep. Do you really sleep through all that or are you just pretending to not hear so that I have to get up every time?"

Luke frowned. "Would I do that to you?"

"Of course, you would, you crumb." She punched him on his shoulder.

"I'm hurt."

"I didn't hit you that hard."

"No, I'm hurt that you would assume that I am so manipulative that I would ignore the cries of our daughter just so you would have to get up."

"But I'm right, aren't I?"

"Yes, but it hurts getting caught. Before you zone out on coffee and my good company, I must tell you about what I just read. There was a large earthquake up in Bellingham this morning. I am going to phone Alan and see how's he's doing."

"Phone him? Maybe you should just text him. He and Maria might not be up yet or," she grinned, "otherwise engaged."

"You're right. I'll text him." Luke picked up his phone and spent several minutes thumbing a text to his best friend, Alan Washington. Shortly after sending the text, Luke's phone rang.

"Hey there, Double O Seven."

"Come on, Alan, what happened with 'what's up, buddy?' And you do know that neither James Bond nor Sean Connery were secret service agents, don't you?"

"Yeah, but yanking your chain is too much fun. Anyway, thanks for the text. Yes, we are all right. We felt the quake, but it wasn't anything that those of us from the Bay Area haven't felt before. Nothing fell apart or fell off or caught fire, so we are all good."

"Good, I just saw the news and got worried. While I have your attention, any chance on the horizon of getting back to sea?"

Alan was Luke's best friend from high school and a baseball teammate. After they both graduated from the Huntington Academy, Alan attended and graduated from the California State University Maritime Academy and was certified as a marine engineer third class. He had worked on the Alaska Ferry and a Maersk container ship, and, finally, achieved his life's ambition landing a job as an engineering officer with Holland America cruise lines. Alan had once told Luke that he was certain he would eventually get a job on a cruise ship, in no small part because he was uncommonly handsome in a dress uniform, skilled at chatting up geriatric cruise ship passengers, and, as an African American, could boost the cruise line's claimed commitment to diversity. His wife, Maria, was a cruise director for Holland America. Just when the stars seemed to be aligned for the couple and they were able to work together on the same ship, COVID-19 came along and sank the cruise industry. They were both furloughed and neither had any immediate prospects of getting back to work. Once furloughed, they decided to rent a condo on Lake Whatcom, near Bellingham, a lake and town Alan learned about when he was with the Alaska Ferry, whose southern terminus is Bellingham, Washington.

"Not with container ships. There are so many engineering officers ashore and looking for work that the competition is really stiff for the few jobs that are available. On a happier note, how are your lovely wife and adorable daughter, neither of which a rogue like you deserves?"

"Thanks for asking; they are fine and, as you say, lovely and adorable. And your lovely bride?"

"She, too, is beautiful and adorable and doing okay. We decided to make good use of this downtime and just found out that she is three months pregnant. Another handsome Washington in on the way. We may have a Christmas baby."

"Wow, congratulations! Annie will be thrilled to hear the news, and I am sure she and Maria will be texting about the whole pregnancy and newborn thing."

"Thanks, Luke. All kidding aside, I know you and Annie are thrilled for us and that means a lot. I have to cut this short, though, as now that Maria is doing all the work of growing our kid, I am officially responsible for breakfast. I better get to it before she accuses me of finding an excuse to avoid my responsibility."

"I can appreciate that fully, buddy. I have the same duty here and can't wait to tell Annie the news. You guys stay well and good luck with the job situation."

"Thanks."

Luke smiled in gratitude of having such a good friend. Each had been each other's best man at their weddings, and though they got together infrequently due to Alan's long stretches at sea, Luke knew that any conversation with Alan was enough to brighten a whole day. Alan was similarly moved and set about making breakfast.

"Okay, you probably figured out what Alan and I were talking about. The two pieces of good news are that they are both all right—the earthquake didn't damage anything or injure anyone in the Washington household—AND they are expecting. Maria is about three months pregnant."

Annie smiled her broad smile. "That's wonderful news. I'll call her later today. They will be great parents and probably have an absolutely beautiful kid." Annie held up her finger for silence and immediately got up and left the kitchen, noting on her way out, "Luke, we really do need to get your hearing checked."

Luke got up to begin preparing breakfast when his phone again chimed a new alert.

> *Bellingham, Washington. 6:49 a.m. PDT. Following a 6.0 earthquake that hit Bellingham, Washington, this morning at 6:36 a.m., one side of a three-story downtown building fell roughly nine feet into what some described as a sinkhole. The other side of the building sank about three feet. Water, power, and gas lines were damaged, but so far, there have been no fires. All utility lines were quickly turned off, and police and fire personnel are currently checking the welfare of the occupants of the four condos in the two top floors of the building. The uneven collapse of the ground under the building resulted in all*

the windows breaking out, the doors being
unhinged, and the structure to split.

Luke texted Alan again: "Just saw the news about a building sinking in Downtown Bellingham. Keep that future mother safe!"

Three

As George walked up Holly Street from breakfast and thought about the work he had to do today: get that cash out of his condo and deposited in several banks, most of which closed at noon on Saturdays. He decided he could probably get it done and have the afternoon free to work on his own internet business when he heard several sirens from adjacent streets. Rounding the corner onto Railroad Avenue, he was struck by the sight of several emergency vehicles—police cars, fire trucks, and ambulances—with blinking lights and dozens of uniformed persons running around and into his building. A large crowd of gawkers had gathered in the middle of Railroad Ave., which had been closed to traffic at each end of his building's block.

What the hell? His building had shrunk by about a floor, at least on one side, while the other side appeared to have sunk a couple of feet into the ground. A large split ran from the ground to the roof, creating about a four-foot gap in the structure at the roof. He saw Maggie, still wearing her robe and wrapped in a wool blanket, sitting on a gurney near an ambulance. He did not see Auggie or the Larsons.

George immediately realized that he was screwed. His condo contained nothing but incriminating evidence: a desk top computer, a laptop, a printer, several boxes of bank records, a couple of digital wallets, and about $30,000 in cash. He could not explain any of them to the police.

George melted into the crowd of spectators to buy some time to figure out what he could do. He saw an immediate future as broken as his building, but he had to try to retrieve his possessions. If he could get them, he could simply drive away and set up shop somewhere else. With considerable trepidation, he approached a uniformed Bellingham police officer who was reeling out yellow police line tape. "Hi, Officer, that's my building. I live in 2A. I need to get in and retrieve some of my stuff."

"Sorry, buddy, no one is going in there now and may not for a long time."

"But, Officer, I am a software developer and have very valuable, irreplaceable work in there."

"Again, we can't allow that right now. Maybe you should go talk with Lieutenant Zale. He is in charge." The officer pointed down the block to a tall man giving directions to another group of officers.

Without any obvious options and realizing that waiting around was going to be dangerous, George approached the lieutenant. "Lieutenant, I was told I needed to talk to you. I live in 2A in that building, and I really need to get some stuff out of there. It is quite valuable."

"2A, you say? And your name is?"

"George Kennedy, and I really need to get into my condo."

"Sorry, sir, I am going to have to ask that you join the other residents over by that aide car and wait until we get a handle on this. I will come tell you all what is going to happen next when I figure it out."

George knew that not only was he not going to get into his condo, but that every minute he stuck around, it was more likely that one of the firemen or police officers crawling all over the building was going to come and ask him some difficult questions. "Okay, sir, I'll wait with the others, but I hope you'll have an answer pretty soon." And he walked through the crowd, not in the direction of Maggie, who was now joined by the Larsons and Auggie, but in the opposite direction, toward his car in a nearby parking garage.

"Lieutenant Zale, I think we have cleared the building of all the occupants. And the buildings on either side. But there is no sign of the occupant of 2A, who, according to the lady over there, is a guy named George Kennedy."

"Actually, I just talked with him. He should be over with the other residents." He looked over to the four and did not see George Kennedy. "Come with me."

Lieutenant Tom Zale approached the quartet of shaken residents and asked Maggie, "Are you okay, ma'am?"

"Oh yeah, I just got my knee and shoulder bunged up a bit when the building fell into that hole. Bounced me around a little, but just bruises, though. I'll be okay."

The lieutenant looked at all four of the blanket-wrapped evacuees. "Have any of you seen George Kennedy?"

"Sure," piped up Maggie. "I saw George right after the quake. We both went outside to check on the exterior of the building. It didn't seem damaged."

"Have you seen him since?"

"No, he said he was going to walk down to the Old Town and have breakfast. I haven't seen him since. Is he okay?"

"Yeah, I talked with him a few minutes ago and he said he was going to come and join you folks and wait for information about when he could get back into his condo. You sure he didn't come this way?"

Maggie and the Larsons shook their heads.

Auggie turned to Harry and yelled, "What did he say?"

Harold Larson leaned closer to Auggie and said loudly, "He was asking if we have seen George."

Auggie shook his head.

"Oh, one more thing," the lieutenant asked. "Does Mr. Kennedy have a car?"

Harry quickly responded, "Oh yeah, a really sweet ride, a 2012 black Mustang GT. He's really proud of it."

"Is there a parking garage for this building?"

"No, George has a monthly lease in the garage down Railroad. So do Maggie and I, for that matter. Auggie doesn't have a car," Harry replied.

"Thanks. Just hang in there a bit. The Red Cross will be here shortly and help you to some temporary housing until we can get his mess straightened out." The lieutenant turned to walk away but abruptly returned to the huddled victims. "One more thing, where does George work?"

Auggie didn't hear the question, but Harry did. "He doesn't. He's a professional gambler, and a pretty damned good one from all the stories he tells."

A fireman and a police officer approached Lieutenant Zale as he walked back to the tent that had been erected in the middle of Railroad Avenue as a temporary command post. The policeman raised a finger to request a minute of his superior's time. "Sir, we have found something a little strange in Apartment 2A. There was literally no furniture, other than a bed, a couple of large folding tables and chairs, two computers, a printer, a couple of apple crates full of what look like bank records, *and* a bunch of money wrapped with rubber bands. It looks like more than twenty-five or thirty grand of cash."

The lieutenant sighed: a missing occupant, and now a bunch of equipment and money in a destroyed building. "Is it safe to go back into that apartment and retrieve that stuff?"

"Above my pay grade, sir, but the city engineer just got here; maybe he can answer your question."

Roy Morgenstern was sixty-four, profoundly thin, and had been the chief engineer for more than twenty-five years. "Howdy, Lieutenant. Some mess, huh?"

"Yeah. What do you think happened here?"

"I'd bet my pension that what we have here is the collapse of a shallow lateral tunnel in the old coal mine that operated under this city years ago. I have been warning people about this for years. More than warning, we have had to deal with subsidence several times in this area, on Holly, Railroad, and State."

"Is this building going to settle or sink any more than it already has?"

"I doubt it, but there are no guarantees."

"Is it safe for my officers to go back in and help retrieve some stuff from the upper floors?"

"Let me do a bit of a walk-around and I'll let you know."

A half an hour later, the city engineer told Lieutenant Tom Zale that he thought it would be safe to send one or two officers into the building, but no more than that and only for a few minutes.

Tom grabbed two handy uniformed officers. "I want you to go into 2A, grab the computers, printer, bank records, and cash, then take all that to the shop and put it in one of the interrogation rooms. Inventory everything you take into custody and get some fingerprints off the computers. Be careful." He was sure it would not be strictly legal to confiscate the requested items, but he believed he could defend his action as preserving personal property in the exigence of an earthquake and a sinkhole, or whatever the hell this mess was. At least, he hoped he could. To buttress his claim for charitable salvaging, he asked yet another officer to go visit the four victims and offer to retrieve important personal items: wallets, purses, eyeglasses, prescription drugs, hearing aids. No televisions, photo albums, clothing, or liquor stash—just important stuff that they would need and couldn't be quickly replaced.

He then signaled for another three uniformed officers and told them, "I want one of you to hustle down to the city parking garage and look for a 2012 black Mustang GT. If you find it, sit on it and let me know. Oh, and wake someone up in city operations and get a license plate number for that car from the parking space lease agreement." A young officer jogged away in the direction of the parking garage. "I want you two to circulate among the spectators and look for a guy— George Kennedy's the name—in his late thirties/early forties, about five-nine, a buck seventy, short brown hair, wearing jeans and a jeans jacket. If you find him, bring him back to me. I have some questions."

*　*　*

It was really sinking into George that he needed to get out of Dodge. The stuff in his unit was a prosecutor's dream treasure trove of evidence. After talking with Lieutenant Zale, and as quickly as he could without attracting attention, he melted through the crowd of spectators that had gathered on Railroad Avenue and worked his way toward the parking garage. Yes, he would simply have to leave town. But—and this was a big "but"—he really didn't want to leave town without his gold. He had almost five pounds of gold bullion coins—about $150,000 worth of American Eagles and Canadian Maple Leafs. The problem was that the gold was in a safety deposit box in one of his banks in Ferndale and it was already 11:40; they closed at noon on Saturdays. They would not be open until Tuesday morning, as Monday was a holiday. So, George decided to get in his car and leave the downtown area, find a motel to hole up in until Tuesday, then grab his gold and leave Bellingham forever.

Four

Late Saturday afternoon, Luke and Annie, with Luke carrying Ashley, walked the couple of blocks from their home to Luke's mother's home for a long-anticipated and often-deferred family dinner. They had all been extremely cautious during the height of the pandemic and had not gotten together in at least ten months. The COVID-19 vaccine rollout had dramatically reduced the spread of the virus, and they had finally decided that all of them could get together for a family dinner. In addition to Luke, Annie, and Ashley, dinner would include his mother and his stepfather, Harrison Holt, as well as; his sister, Larissa, her husband, Henry, and their eight-year-old son, Jason. Annie and Larissa's husband had gotten the vaccine as essential workers; she was a speech therapist, and he, a social worker, both in the public schools. Annie had been the luckier of the two, as she had been able to continue her therapy sessions with her student clients during the shutdown via Zoom, though not all her clients in the schools had had the needed technology or the family commitment to continue with the sessions remotely. Henry had simply been laid off. Luke had gotten the vaccine as a law enforcement officer, while his mother, Elizabeth, had been vaccinated as a health care worker, though she had retired a year ago. Harrison had an underlying condition—high cholesterol—so he had been vaccinated early on, though Liz had to plead with him to claim the priority. Among the adults, only Larissa had yet to be vaccinated, but in her effort to protect Jason, she had worked exclusively from home as a venture capital advisor and literally had no personal contact with anyone for almost a year.

As they approached the front door of his mother's place, Luke had the same strange feeling he felt whenever he returned to this house. He had grown up in this house, and he and Annie had lived there for two years when they were first married and before Harrison had shown up. It just seemed strange to knock on the door that, for many years, he just unlocked and walked through.

Liz heard the doorbell and ran to the front door. "Luke, Annie, and Ashley, come in, come in. I am so glad we can finally get together." She proceeded to hug Luke and Annie with a vigor that belied her slender build but reflected the strain of long absence. She then held out her arms and took Ashley from Luke and smothered her in kisses, then held her on her hip like she might not give her up for the entire evening.

"There's a scene I have longed to see!" Harrison walked into the entryway and shook Luke's hand, hugged Annie, and a patted Ashley on the head as she snuggled to her grandmother's chest.

Luke was close to tears of happiness, so, for both himself and everyone else, tried an airy response, "Howdy, Harrison, we are so glad to see you all and to finally be able to get together."

Larissa, Henry, and Jason joined the family gathering in the hallway. Long-avoided hugs, kisses, and tears of happiness were shared.

Finally, Liz, still holding tight to Ashley, said loudly, "Okay, Okay, we don't need to all stand around out here. Come in, come in."

The family had a well-appointed living room but seldom, if ever, used it except to watch television. They all knew that family life in this house centered in the large kitchen, so that was where they all migrated.

Annie saw a full pot of freshly brewed coffee and went to pour herself a cup. "Anyone else want some coffee?"

Luke and Harrison both said, "Yes, thank you."

Larissa headed for the stove. "I'll make Henry and I some tea. Mom, do you want some tea?"

"No, thanks, I think I'll have my usual." She headed for the refrigerator for a Diet Coke.

Everyone seemed to all be speaking at once, so anxious were they to catch up and reconnect, but eventually, they sorted themselves out along predictable lines. Liz, Annie, and Larissa stayed in the kitchen, sitting down with their drink of choice at the scarred but comforting large kitchen table, with Ashley still in her grandmother's arms and Jason retreating to the play area in the corner of the kitchen, which Liz had built when Jason and Larissa had first returned to the family home. Luke, Henry, and Harrison went into the living room to watch the Giants and Dodgers' game, already tied in the top of the sixth.

Larissa turned to Annie with a huge smile and declared, "Annie, it is so good to see you. Those Zoom chats just suck. You look great! You're so toned and athletic. I was fat after Jason for more than a year."

"I give Luke a lot of credit. Just days after Ashley was born, he had me out walking while he would carry little miss in a chest carrier. Luke came home from his basic training in the best condition of his life and really wanted to stay in shape too. After a while, we started jogging slowly and we bought a three-wheeled stroller that Luke can push at a trot. Jogging around outside and staying away from people has really been all we can do for exercise these days, so that's what we've been doing over the last couple of months."

Liz inwardly smiled at the banter between her daughter and her daughter-in-law. Larissa had re-entered their lives at the memorial service for her grandfather, after a troubled and dangerous decade of drugs and living on the streets. She showed up with a child, a wonderful young man, who would soon become her husband, and a college degree. Annie and Larissa had become close, to Liz's great satisfaction. She roused herself from her introspection. "Hon, has Henry gotten any word about when school is going to fully reopen and he can get back to work?"

"Actually, he has. Just yesterday, he got an email that the schools are going to open Monday, August 2, and he will be on the payroll and is expected at his school on that day."

Annie hoisted her coffee in a salute. "I got the same note. They are starting in early August because they have added twenty days to the school year. It will now be two hundred days, rather than the usual one hundred and eighty. Both the teacher and staff unions are squawking about it because there is not going to be any increases in salary, but I think almost everyone agrees the extension is a good idea. The kids will inevitably have some making up to do after a year of remote instruction."

"How about you?" Liz asked her daughter, as she stroked her granddaughter's wispy hair, "Are you going to be going into the office pretty soon or continue to work from home?"

"Actually, the office really isn't necessary for the most important part of my work. I can do the research and paperwork as well from home as from the office but getting out into the businesses and startups to do our due diligence is the real challenge. When people are comfortable enough to allow strangers in and talking to all their people, then things will return to normal for us. However, I hear that the partners are talking about seriously downsizing our office presence to save some of the extremely high overhead costs of maintaining a large downtown office and having most of us associates work from home permanently."

Annie looked at the clock on the wall and asked Liz, "Okay, Liz, what can we do to help get dinner ready and on the table?"

"I've planned a pretty simple dinner: ham, salad, peas and carrots, and baked potatoes, and mac and cheese for Jason. And a store-bought apple pie with ice cream for dessert. You could set the table and maybe ask Harrison what wine he wants from his cellar."

Annie leaned into the hallway to the living room and yelled, "Okay, gentlemen, you are on notice. Dinner is underway and will be served in about an hour, after which you three are totally in charge of the kitchen! Harrison, Liz asked me to suggest that you retrieve whatever wine you want from the cellar."

Luke, Harrison, and Henry looked at each other and broke out laughing. Luke expressed their shared reaction to the trumpeted challenge. "I think we've been told that we have the clean-up duty after dinner and we have enough time before dinner to see the end of this game."

Harrison went to his wine cellar in garage to gather his preferred wine.

When he returned, Luke asked, "So, Harrison, how badly affected was the foundation by the pandemic?" Harrison was the founder and CEO of the Holt

Foundation for the Advancement of Personal Finance Literacy and the Promotion of Public Policy Ensuring Financial Security.

"We got hammered on several fronts, and we've also learned some things. With schools being shut down all over the country, teachers trying to learn how to teach remotely, and school boards cherry about public meetings, there is almost no momentum left for schools adopting financial literacy curriculum. Our teach-the-teachers activities have almost ground to a halt. My work as the principal fundraiser for the foundation has also been slammed. Fundraising is a person-to-person, glad-handing, and schmoozing activity—none of which has been possible for months. But we have learned that our curriculum developers need to work on a whole portfolio of online lessons and activities that teachers and school districts can literally just take off the shelves and use. Even when all this virus situation is behind us, those will be valuable resources that we did not have before. However, Luke, I must tell you, Edith Washington has been a valuable addition to our staff. I can't tell you how much I appreciate you getting us together. She just finished a one-hundred-page book, titled *It's YOUR Money*, that is tied to the financial literacy curriculum we have developed. A friend of mine who owns a publishing business volunteered to put the book out for actual cost, meaning that districts can get it for just under nine bucks a pop. Bottom line is that she is a real gem and seems to be mightily enjoying the work."

"I had a feeling that you two would hit it off. I will pass your compliment onto Alan. I am sure he will be delighted but probably not surprised that his mother is a valued colleague."

Henry told Luke and Harrison about the recall to active duty in open schools, for which Luke and Harrison offered congratulations and Harrison privately thanked the heavens for news that the schools were about to begin to return to normal.

Henry pointed to the television and exclaimed, "How is it that they can't turn a simple double play like that!" Henry was a generally quiet young man, an Afghanistan war veteran, a great husband to Larissa and father to Jason, and a caring professional who worked tirelessly with students to help them overcome social and familial impediments to their education. Though he was much more a football fan than a baseball zealot, he appreciated any competition on any type of field or court.

Luke chuckled. "Henry, I think your heart got in the way of your eyes on that one. I've been involved in hundreds of attempted double plays, and they are not as easy as they might look from the comfort of our seats in the stands or at home."

"I know, but, really, that one looked like the so-called 'tailor-made double play' opportunity."

"You are right, it was, and you are right, they blew it. I suspect they will hear about that when they get into the dugout."

Jason ran into the living room and jumped up on the couch between Henry and Harrison. Harrison loved having Jason living in their home; it was the chance to watch and help a child grow up that he had not experienced before he married Liz and moved into the house. Harrison tossed Jason's hair. "You want to watch some baseball, big guy?"

"Yep. Mom, Grandma, and Aunt Annie just talk and talk and talk. Who's winning?"

The timing could not have been better. Literally moments after the game concluded, which the Giants won with a walk-off double in the bottom of the ninth, Annie called the males to dinner.

As Liz had suspected, the meal was not the attraction of the hour-and-half family dinner; the conversations, stories, laughing, and easy teasing were. Liz smiled when Jason asked if he could be excused and, when released from the adult banter, headed directly into the kitchen to play with the new computer game Liz had gotten him. There was so much for the family to catch up with each other.

Harrison asked Luke, "So, Luke, you haven't said much about your work."

"Same old, same old: investigate, catch the bad guy, investigate some more, testify, and repeat."

"Oh, come on, you must have some good crook tales you can share." Everyone looked at Luke expectantly; none of them had ever heard an actual crook story from Luke.

"I'm sorry, I really can't go into any current cases and the old ones are, well, just that, old. However, I have learned a couple of things that really surprised me. First, before joining the Service, I never suspected that most of the investigative work would done from my desk, especially in the financial end of crimes. You can't avoid leaving trails when dealing with money, and following the crumbs is actually a highly effective way of getting to the bottom of crime. As they say, 'Follow the money,' which today is usually just carefully following electronic trails. I've also learned that the television and movie portrayal of interagency jealousies and infighting is malarkey. I guess it used to be that way, but after 9/11, the various federal and local law enforcement agencies have really learned to work together rather well and I have never seen one of them, like the FBI, come in and big foot their way into controlling an investigation. In fact, about six months ago, I got appointed as one of the Secret Service representatives on the Joint Task Force on cryptocurrency crimes that includes every alphabet law enforcement agency you have ever heard of: FBI, NSA, DEA, IRS, SEC, CIA, DIA, and a few others I can't recall. My role on the JTF is mostly as a forensic accountant."

Liz beamed. "Who better to be a forensic accountant than a young man who graduated in accounting and passed the CPA and then graduated law school and passed the bar?"

"Mom, you'll recall that bar thing took two tries."

"Yes, but you did pass."

"Cryptocurrency crimes? Like in Bitcoin?" Henry wondered out loud.

"Yeah, Bitcoin and Ethereum, and about twelve hundred other cryptocurrencies."

"But those alternative currencies are, in themselves, not illegal," noted Harrison.

"No, but they have become the currency of choice in a whole range of illegal activities, like financing international terrorism, drug and sex trafficking, money laundering, and tax evasion. They also get hacked and stolen. Cryptocurrencies are also used in phony alternative currency offerings and Ponzi schemes. But, in my experience, most of the people who buy alt currencies, like Bitcoins, do so as a speculation or investment, just like some people buy gold and silver. The price of these things is highly volatile—this year alone Bitcoins have sold for as little as six thousand and as much as sixty-five thousand, so speculators or traders can and have made lots of money if they bought and sold at the right time. They have also lost a heck of a lot of money."

Harrison noted, "I lived through the dot com bubble and the sub-prime mortgage meltdown and read about the Dutch tulip bulb fiasco. It sounds like Bitcoins are just another speculative bubble that will someday simply burst, leaving a whole lot of people out in the financial cold."

Larissa smiled. "I remember hearing about that Dutch tulip bulb mania in one of my finance classes. If I remember it correctly, in the sixteen hundreds, speculation in bulbs for new tulip varieties got so hot that, one day, a single bulb sold for something like ten times what the average Dutch worker earned in a year. The investors who had driven up the prices turned to each other and said, 'This is really stupid.' In a matter of days, the price for bulbs fell ninety-nine percent."

Harrison remembered one more detail about the Dutch tulip bulb bubble. "The funny thing is that the only reason people know about the tulip bulb mania is the publication of a hyperbolic book by a Scottish journalist in the eighteen hundreds with a title I always remembered because it sounded appropriate to our own times: *Extraordinary Popular Delusions and the Madness of Crowds*."

Liz said, "I know nothing about tulip bulb prices, but I have seen Bitcoin vending machines in shopping malls, so it would appear that they have become mainstream. Can you actually go into a store and buy a new television with Bitcoins?"

Luke quickly responded, "In a small but rapidly increasing number of retail stores, yes, you can. In fact, I read a story the other day that reported that Tesla may soon accept Bitcoins for the purchase of their cars."

"But why?" Henry asked. "If you have six hundred in cash to buy a television, why would you convert it to Bitcoin just to spend them in the store?"

"As I said, only a small percentage of Bitcoin purchasers actually intend to spend them—except in those illegal markets like drugs and weapons. Most are investors. Some high-tech zealots are attracted to cryptocurrencies because they love the underlying block chain technology. Another group, basically libertarians and those who don't trust the government, are fearful that the Federal Reserve and Congress are manipulating the national currency or that the greenback is going to collapse in value, and they want to own these alternative currencies."

Larissa replied, "We have seen an increasing number of our deals involving Bitcoins. We really aren't set up for them and their wild fluctuations in value often mess up deals that might take weeks to put together, but we can't turn away from a deal just because it involves Bitcoins. We had one case where an investor put up around ten million dollars' worth of Bitcoins for a specific percentage of the company, and by the time the paperwork was completed, the value of the investment to the company had shrunk to eight million dollars and they wanted to renegotiate the percentage of the company involved in the deal. Bottom line is that the whole deal fell apart before closing."

Annie saw that a much longer conversation could easily develop, so she got up from the table, lifted Ashley from her high-chair, and took her into the den to privately feed her daughter.

Liz turned to Larissa and suggested, "Larissa, our work is done here. Let's you and I go for a walk down to Marina Green and leave the men to their duties." They quickly headed for the front door while Luke, Henry, and Harrison began to pick up glasses, dishes, serving platters, and silverware and carried them into the kitchen.

Luke took charge of the sink to rinse and place items in the dishwasher, Harrison transferred the left-over food into plastic refrigerator storage containers and succeeded in gobbling down the small last piece of pie in the process. Henry continued to ferry items from the dining room. With the dishwasher full, Luke washed the remaining plates, bowels, cups, glasses, and silver while Henry and Harrison dried and put the clean dishes in their correct cupboards and shelves. As they worked, Henry and Harrison continued to question Luke about the whole phenomena that was cryptocurrency.

Henry was genuinely puzzled. "I guess I really don't get it. People buy these alternative currencies, but their value or purchasing power are still measured in dollars AND they pay commission costs going into and getting out of them. What's the point?"

Luke smiled inwardly; he had exactly the same question. "Henry, I agree completely. The greenback is backed only by the 'full faith and credit of the United Sates' and most of these alt currencies seem to be backed by nothing other than what the current fickle speculators think they are worth—just smoke, like the greenback, but more subject to the whims of the market than is the dollar. The additional problem is that the government reporting and regulatory environment simply hasn't caught up with the reality of cryptocurrencies on the ground. The IRS says they are an asset or a commodity and any gains from trading in them must be reported as a capital gain, but there is no systemwide reporting requirement to alert the government that a gain has been made. The securities and exchange commission has declined to say there are securities, like a stock, but they have prosecuted people for offering phony cryptos under provisions of securities fraud. Estimates are that literally billions of dollars in state and local taxes are avoided—or evaded—by conducting commerce and investing in alt currencies. The whole environment has been called the 'Wild West' and is badly in need of legislative involvement."

Harrison concluded the discussion for all of them with, "I guess I really don't get it, but what if they are right and the dollar hits the skids? I imagine most of us would wish we had some cryptocurrencies or gold or a collection of fine wines."

As the men were surveying their success with their job, Annie walked in carrying Ashley on her hip. "Well, looks like you guys did a great job cleaning up. I am sure Liz and Larissa will be as happy to know guys have such a skill set; it could be useful. Where are they, by the way?"

Luke told his wife, "They took a walk down toward the park, but they should be back pretty soon."

"Okay, but I think we should consider going home pretty soon. Ashley is about to crash for the night, and if she falls asleep here, we might wake her up going home later and she won't settle down again after that."

"I'll get our coats in just a minute. Let's wait until Mom and Larissa get back." Luke turned and shook Henry's and Harrison's hands and gave each a quick back-slapping hug. "Great working with you guys. Actually, it was great...to finally see you in person." He went over to Jason, playing on the floor, and put up his palm for a high-five, which Jason obliged by slapping palms. "Good to see you, little man. Pretty soon we'll have you over to our house and I'll show some secret hiding places that Aunt Annie doesn't even know about." That evinced a smile, an "okay," and hug from Jason.

Larissa and Liz walked into the kitchen, and in her mock stricken voice, Liz exclaimed, "What, you three are leaving already?" Annie explained about Ashley's sleep schedule, and Liz grudgingly admitted the wisdom of the decision but not without again taking Ashley in her arms and smothering her in kisses.

It took another ten minutes for the young Bitterman family to make it out the door and on their way home. "I think I told you that when we moved out, Mom told me she wasn't looking forward to living in the house alone for the first time ever. And now look at her. She and Harrison act like a couple of love-struck twenty-year-olds. Mom obviously loves having Larissa and Henry living there, and she dotes on Jason. She went from a prospect of an empty house to a full house. It couldn't have worked out better. I don't think I have seen her so happy—ever."

"Lucas Wallace Bitterman, you are a good son and a hopeless romantic, and I love you for it... as does little miss."

***

Saturday George had left Bellingham, still in a panic and without much of plan about what to do next, except that he needed to retrieve his gold on Tuesday. He had driven south on I-5 with no idea where he was going, only that he needed to get away from all those prying cops and firemen. As he passed Lake Samish, he began to calm down and decided that he would find a motel somewhere and go to an electronics store to buy a new computer and a couple of digital wallets. In his leather wallet, he had a copy of the cheat sheet he had taped to the bottom of his printer. If he could get new digital wallets, he could use the personal signature and seed words to both reestablish his accounts in the new wallets and wipe clean the ones orphaned in his condo.

George pulled into a rest stop and used his phone to determine the location of a nearby electronics store. The closest was in Bellingham. That would not work. The next closest was in Mount Vernon. Though the Mount Vernon store did not have the exact model of the wallets in his condo, they did have a lower-priced version of the same brand, so he bought two and a new laptop. He then went to Walmart and bought some clothes, toiletries, and an inexpensive briefcase.

Five

Early Sunday morning, Lieutenant Tom Zale parked behind the police department headquarters on Grand Avenue and used a key card for the employee entrance door to enter the building. He walked through the main bullpen of desks and offices, waving to a couple of officers at work, as he made his way to Interrogation Room 2.

The room contained all the items he had requested be taken from Unit 2A the day before and a neatly printed inventory, stating:

> *– one desk-top computer, with a broken*
> *monitor screen, and all cables, unexamined*
> *– one laptop computer, unexamined*
> *– one printer and all connecting cables*

— two boxes of bank records, unexamined
— two hardware digital
wallets, unexamined
— six bundles of cash, totaling $29,345
— one sheet of paper, taped to the bottom of
the computer, unexamined

Tom put on a pair of nitrile gloves and picked up the paper that had been taped to the bottom of the computer.

1BvDr278Pqst4Bl0lr2BMldqAc56LpIU6f5

5KlO0Pq1vc745g66IkcDv8rL

Cow verb bleed income open ice best
yellow auto canter flash tire

1rT8Bn08Gf49Mqe4X90LvR16fqxO0fRDp7

1R9rnl9Sqp3y6L0m2z3D19Rv8w1Di1Mn0

Hp023cCuIn3VxC5iQlPvN31SL

Red corn plead sky truck fire lever
clash goat hope horse pink

916-211-4867

360-881-0821

Tom put the paper back on the table and took off his gloves when Officer Jim Hines knocked and entered room, "Hi, Lieutenant, I heard you were down here. As you can see, I retrieved and inventoried the stuff you wanted from that condo."

"Yes, yes, Jim, you did a good job here, but for the life of me, I can't figure out what it all means."

"Well, I may have some more information to further confuse the situation. You asked me to take prints from the computer and the printer, and I got a hit. All the prints belong to a Roger Simpson and—"

Tom interrupted, "Not to a George Kennedy?"

"Nope, all the prints belong to this Roger Simpson AND there is an outstanding warrant for his arrest. Roger Simpson, aka George Kennedy, was arrested for identify theft in Sacramento, arraigned, and was ROR'd but failed to appear at his trial. We also got the city folks to finally get us a license plate for that black Mustang. The plate actually belongs to a 2009 Honda Accord, which was crushed in a wrecking yard in Mount Vernon more than a year ago."

Tom smiled at Jim in hopes that he would understand he was being light in what he said, "Well, Officer Hines, you have certainly been busy and have, indeed, made my day more complicated."

Officer Hines grinned back at his superior. "We do what we can, sir. Anything else I can help you with?"

"No, that's fine. Have you been home since yesterday?"

"No, I wanted to be sure to have everything ready when you came in."

"Well, go home. Get some sleep. Watch a ballgame. Have a beer. I'll see you tomorrow."

"Thanks, sir. I'll definitely work on all those tasks. See you tomorrow."

Tom pulled out a chair and tried to figure out just what the hell he was dealing with: a broken building; a guy calling himself George Kennedy, who actually was Roger Simpson and wanted in Sacramento; a black Mustang with stolen plates; a pile of cash; and a bunch of bank records. And whatever those computers and digital wallets contained. It had all the appearance of a money-laundering operation, but laundering money from what? The most likely was that the cash and the money being handled in those digital accounts was from drug activity, but there were no drugs or guns found in the condo, the two items most often linked with a drug operation. This, he concluded, was not going to ruin what was left of his weekend. He had plans to take his family to his parents' house in Ferndale for a Sunday family dinner. He pulled out his phone and phoned his captain to explain the situation.

"Well, Tom, I imagine your thinking that this is a drug and money-laundering operation is probably right. Let me tell the chief and see what he thinks we should do. I suspect that this Roger Simpson is in the wind, but I'll leave that call to the chief. At least the earthquake or building collapse shut down whatever was going on there."

"You know, Captain, the part that really pisses me off is that I actually talked with him, but I just didn't have any reason to suspect he was any more than a victim of the building collapse. I honestly felt sorry for him because he told me he had some valuable stuff in his unit that he really wanted to retrieve."

"Don't worry about it, Tom. You couldn't have known, and we may never know. I will let you know what the chief says. Have a good rest of the weekend."

He planned to.

After the report from the captain, the chief of police phoned a long-time friend who was based in the FBI's Seattle office. He also put out a BOLO for a 2012 black Mustang with the stolen plate number and the description of Roger Simpson, aka George Kennedy, wanted for a failure-to-appear bench warrant and suspected of drug dealing and money laundering.

Six

On Sunday morning, Luke slept in. During the night, he had heard Ashley fussing and told Annie to stay in bed, then went to rock his daughter back to sleep. When he woke up in morning, Annie was already out of bed and he heard her gently singing to Ashley downstairs. Maybe he had a won a few points—at least the option to sleep in—by getting up during the night. His phone rang on the bedside table; the caller ID informed Luke that it was Neal Hanson, the special agent in charge of the San Francisco Field Office of the Secret Service.

"Good morning, boss. What's up?"

"Luke, I am sorry to bother you on a Sunday morning and ruin your holiday weekend, but I need you to put on your JTF hat and make a trip today."

"Where to, boss?"

Luke and Neal Hanson had a friendly relationship. Luke had met Neal almost three years earlier when Luke was trying to figure out what to do with a problematic inheritance from his grandfather, a 1933 Saint-Gaudens Double Eagle gold coin. As Luke learned, the coin was illegal to own but likely worth more than seven million dollars. Luke met Neal to determine what the Secret Service's position would be about the famous coin being donated to the Museum of Modern Art. After a long conversation over drinks and dinner, Neal had gone out of his way to encourage Luke to join the Secret Service. Since coming back to San Francisco after his basic training, Luke enjoyed working with and for Neal and Neal had been appreciative of the accounting and legal expertise Luke brought to the job.

"Bellingham, Washington. The police up there found evidence of what looks like a money-laundering scheme in an apartment that was ruined when the apartment building collapsed into a sink hole or something. The occupant of the apartment in question apparently took flight. Anyway, the locals called the FBI, who called me requesting your forensic accounting expertise to help sort out the situation. They have also called in Sara Donovan from the DEA, and you are to meet her in the office of a Lieutenant Zale of the Bellingham Police Department Monday morning at nine."

"Sara Donovan; that's cool. I worked with her on the Sherwood case about six months ago. She is a real byte witch."

"A what?"

"Byte witch. That's what one of the techies on the Sherwood case called her. She is an IT savant. She can do anything with a computer and a keyboard. Anyway, I look forward to working with her again."

"That's a rich one... 'byte witch.'... I will have to remember that. We have booked a flight on Alaska for you for three-thirty this afternoon out of SFO for Sea-Tac. There are ongoing flights from Seattle up to Bellingham, but the connections are so lousy, we only booked you into Seattle. You'll have to rent a car and drive up to Bellingham."

"No problem, boss. It's funny, just yesterday I talked with my best friend who happens to live in Bellingham. I might just crash at his place while I investigate this money-laundering thing. Any idea about how long I should plan on being up there?"

"No, just the usual—as long as it takes. By the way, Suzie already filed the TSA pre-clearance for your weapon. All you will have to do is show your credentials and sign the paperwork when you check in with Alaska."

"Okay. Alaska Airlines three-thirty this afternoon, Lieutenant Zale and Agent Donovan in Zale's office, and figure out a money-laundering operation. Got it."

"That's it, Luke. Please apologize to Annie for me for messing up your weekend and shuffling you out of town."

"Will do."

Luke walked into the kitchen to find Annie sitting on the floor and entertaining Ashley in her rocking kid carrier, which had rattles and stuffed animals, and Annie making a bunch of odd sounds that Ashley obviously thought were hilarious. "Unless you are teaching her a language I am not familiar with, you might switch to English so she can actually go to college someday."

Annie threw a small stuffed lion at Luke, turned to Ashley, pointed at Luke, and said, "Carraaggto huh some bo bo." Ashley laughed.

"Very funny, mug-a-wah-do-do. If you wouldn't mind switching to English for a minute, I must tell you about a call I just got from Neal. I have to go out of town this afternoon, but it will not be all bad because I am being sent up to Bellingham."

"What? The Secret Service investigates earthquakes now?"

"Actually, kind of. The earthquake and the building that collapsed into that sink hole unearthed what looks to be an illegal operation that had been operating in the building. The JTF was called, and Sara Donovan of the DEA and I are going to meet there and try to sort it out."

"Is Sara Donovan cute?"

"Yes, but not as cute as you and Ashley."

"Okay, you can go. When do you have to leave?"

"I have a flight out of SFO at three-thirty this afternoon. I'll call for an Uber ride around two this afternoon."

"Well, that will put a crimp in our plans to get together with Margie and her husband." Margie was a speech pathology colleague, and she and Annie had become friends when they were in graduate school. Their friendship deepened when both women ended up working for the schools and each had her first child at about the same time. Luke liked Margie's husband, David, and had looked forward to the afternoon and early dinner.

"Sorry, hon. But, you know, you don't have to miss getting together with Margie and David; you and Ashley could just go without me."

Annie brightened. "I might just do that. Keep an eye on little miss while I go up, get a shower, and change. Remember she is beginning to really motor with that tummy scoot of hers."

Luke got a cup of coffee and entertained Ashley with sounds from his newly learned language. Ashley seemed to understand. Luke decided he should switch back to English when he phoned Alan.

"Good morning, buddy. Long time no hear. Oh yeah, we just talked yesterday."

"If twice in two days is too much for you, I can hang up and phone Maria."

"No, I can deal with it. What's up?"

"Turns out I am coming your way this afternoon."

"To Bellingham? Why? Not that I don't look forward to seeing you."

"I have been asked to come up and investigate an apparent crime scene uncovered when that downtown building collapsed."

"What time will you be getting in? I can pick you up."

"Actually, I'm flying into Seattle and going to rent a car and drive to Bellingham. I should be getting into town around eight or eight-thirty. I was hoping I could crash with you guys for a night or two."

"Sure, no problem. It will be great to have a chance to actually talk in person."

"Is eight or nine too late to arrive for you guys?"

"Again, no problem. We have been binge watching the entire *Longmire* series, so we will be up and looking forward to greeting you at Casa Washington."

"Great. I'll see you this evening then."

"'Till then, buddy."

At 1:30 in the afternoon, Luke, carrying a bowl of salad and a small chocolate cake in a wicker basket, and Annie, carrying Ashley in the baby carrier, went to their single-car garage. They had a new Honda CRV that Annie loved to drive, and Luke had grudgingly admitted served their purposes. His beloved 1953 MG TD, a graduation gift from his grandfather, had simply proved to be inadequate for the three of them and unserviceable in hauling groceries, diaper bags, mountain bikes, or surfboards. Luke had wanted to get a Chevy Tahoe, but when he took a measuring tape to the narrow, single-car garage at his house, he realized it simply would not fit. The TD had to go and the

Tahoe wouldn't fit, so a compact recreational vehicle that was big enough to actually haul family and things and small enough to park in their own garage was the answer. He did not have to like it, but he understood they had little choice.

Luke leaned into the open driver's side window and kissed his wife. "Apologize for me to Margie and David, and you and little miss have a good time. I will call you when I get to Alan's house. Love you," he said, then brightly mumbled something in his new language to Ashley, who again seemed to understand and laughed.

***

The flight to Seattle was an eye-opener for Luke. He had never traveled further north on the West Coast than Ashland, when he, his wife, and mother attended plays at the Oregon Shakespeare Festival. Luke had a window seat and saw a spectacular view of Mount Shasta from 34,000 feet and, later, of Mount Hood east of Portland and near the Columbia River, followed by the decapitated Mount Saint Helens. As they descended on approach to Sea-Tac, he was awed by the view of Mount Rainier.

The elderly man sitting next to Luke observed, "Pretty impressive, isn't it?"

Luke turned, "Oh yeah, that is some mountain."

"About forty years and fifty pounds ago, I actually climbed that puppy."

"Really? That must have been hard. How high is it?"

"Fourteen thousand four hundred and eleven feet. It is an active volcano. It doesn't look like it is showing off today, but sometimes you can see steam coming off the top of the mountain. And, yes, it is a tough climb. The top you see there aren't just snow fields, they are glaciers, and crossing them on the way up or down can be dangerous. Several people die each year climbing that mountain. The other thing about that mountain, compared to the other peaks in the continental US, is that the entirety of the mountain rises from low foothills—all fourteen thousand feet of it. But the mountain makes weather forecasting amazingly easy."

Luke looked at the man quizzically.

"Yeah, you see, weather forecasters simply have to tell people, 'Look out your window. If you can't see the mountain, it is raining; if you can, it is going to.'"

The plane turned on approach to Sea-Tac and Luke lost his view of Rainier. His tour guide asked, "So what brings you to the beautiful northwest?"

"Oh, I have some business in Bellingham."

"Bellingham, yep, that is one pretty town. My wife got her degree in home economics up at Western. Did you know that Bellingham is the northernmost town of over fifty thousand residents in the continental US? Or that Bellingham is north of Victoria, British Columbia?"

"No, I didn't."

"Not only that, but did you know that there is a section of Whatcom County, that's the county in which Bellingham sits, that can only be reached by driving through Canada?"

"I didn't know that either."

"Well, it's a long story, but the 49th parallel, which Britain and the US agreed would be the border, ended up cutting off a five-square-mile piece of the Tsawwassen peninsula and giving it to the United States. Today, it is called Point Roberts and can only be reached by driving about twenty-five miles through Canada."

Luke was glad the plane was landing.

Seven

Luke's plane landed at Sea-Tac right on time. He went directly to the car rental desk and was soon on Interstate 5, headed into and through Seattle, on his way to Bellingham. The Sunday afternoon traffic was light. As he drove by the University of Washington campus, he thought of his stepfather, Harrison, who had gotten his undergraduate degree at the sprawling campus and of the director of the Museology program, with whom he had chatted as he tried to determine what to do with his problematic inheritance three years earlier.

Luke passed through Everett and noted the freeway bridge had crossed the Snohomish River. A few minutes later, he saw a freeway exit sign for the Tulalip Reservation, confirming his speculation that many of the place names in this part of the world derived from the Native Americans who had preceded the white set-tlers by thousands of years. He smiled as the highway north took him over the Stillaguamish, Skagit, and Samish rivers.

Luke followed the directions from his phone's GPS. They unerringly took him right to Alan and Maria's rented condo on the shore of Lake Whatcom. Luke was surprised how long the summer days were up here, which was only two-and-half hours of flight time north of San Francisco. He parked in a marked visitor spot in the building's ground floor parking garage and grabbed his small suitcase from the back seat. At the elevator, he saw a row of call buttons and a speaker. He pressed the button for 3A and Alan quickly answered, "I'll send the elevator down. Just leave the pizza on the floor and send it up to the third floor. I'll catch your tip the next time round."

"Sorry, sir, you still owe me tips for the last four times we went through this routine. I am coming up to deliver my pizza and collect my FIVE tips."

"Okay, okay, be that way. I'll send the eleva-tor down."

When the elevator door opened on the third floor, Alan and Maria were standing in the hallway in front of their rented condo, huge grins on their handsome faces, and Alan waving ten one-dollar bills. They all hugged in the hallway, and Alan led them into the condo. "Come out on the deck. We just finished with Episode Seven of Season Two and have some beer on ice to celebrate."

Alan handed Luke a cold bottle of Rainier beer. The view from the veranda was stunning. The long sunset lit the lake and the lights from the houses and condos along the edge of the lake were beginning to reflect off the calm surface of Lake Whatcom.

"This is beautiful, guys," Luke said. The lake seemed to stretch into the mountains and the evergreens surrounding it. "How long is this lake?"

"It's about ten miles long and averages about a mile in width, so it is a fairly good size lake, certainly larger than Lake Spreckels. Have a seat and tell us all about Annie, Ashley, Liz, Harrison, Larissa, your work, the life and times of being a Double O Seven agent, what brings you to Bellingham, how long you can stay, why you don't text me more often, and if you have seen my mom or dad lately."

"Well, good, great, fine, handsome, interesting, and...what were the other questions? Oh, yeah, I have seen your mom and dad lately. I made a Costco run about a month ago and ran into them there. Your mom looked great and said she really enjoys working at Harrison's foundation. Harrison, by the way, just yesterday told me that hiring your mom was one of the best decisions he had ever made and that she just finished writing a book about personal finance. Your dad looked good too. He has lost some weight since last time I saw him, and he was walking smoothly with his prosthetic."

"We talk on the phone or do a Zoom chat about twice a week," added Maria, "and, you're right, they do seem to be doing fine, though I am a little surprised you saw them out and about, as they have been assiduously careful during this damned pandemic."

"Excuse me a moment, guys. I need to phone Annie and let her know I arrived safely." He went into the living room and phoned his wife. "Hi, love, I am safely here with Alan and Maria. How was your visit with Margie and David?"

"It was great. They are doing fine. They missed you. Their little Ricky is a hoot. He is ten months old now, and he and Ashley seemed to socialize. He is beginning to pull himself up on the coffee table and stand up. He takes a tentative step or two, falls on his padded behind, and laughs like crazy. Every time he did that, Ashley laughed too and did her semi-crawling, stomach-scoot thing. They were fun to watch together. How are Alan and Maria?"

"Let me go out on the deck and put you on speaker phone. They'd love to say hi."

Luke put his phone on the table and turned on the phone speaker. "Hi, guys, how the heck are you?"

Maria was the first to respond. "We're doing great. How is that adorable daughter of yours... and you doing?"

"We're both fine. Sick and tired of the social isolation, but that will hopefully end soon. Thank you for taking in my husband; he's not very good at taking care of himself when he is on the road, and it is reassuring that he is with responsible adults."

"Wait a minute! I resemble that!"

"Well, guys, I have to go. I have another call and it is probably my boyfriend asking if the coast is clear. Love you all." She hung up before anyone could respond.

"She probably did have another call—from her mother, who phones about this time three or four nights a week. They are close and haven't seen each other for more than a year now."

"Luke, we can catch up on all kinds of stuff over the next few days, but since you are here about something revealed by that earthquake and the building collapse, you got to know that people up here have been freaking out. Turns out that what happened to that building was that it sank, unevenly, because it and the ground underneath it fell into a tunnel from an old coal mine. The local television and radio stations and the newspaper have been wall-to-wall background information about the mines underneath virtually all of Bellingham. Most long-term residents of Bellingham knew about the tunnels, but either forgot about them or didn't think anything like what happened would happen."

Maria added, "With time on our hands, we have watched or read pretty much everything the media have put out about the mines, the experts they have interviewed, and the freak-out reactions of many of the citizens. Not much else is being discussed around Bellingham."

"If I understand this situation correctly," said Alan as he passed a bowl of pretzels to Luke, "there were lots of coal mines in this area. The biggest one, the Bellingham Coal Mine, left more than two hundred miles of tunnels under the north end of town. Turns out that the tunnels were simply what miners dug out as they chased the seams of coal that ran laterally from the shafts. The shafts were vertical, running to the surface and were used to haul out the coal and ferry workers and supplies up and down into the tunnels. But that mine was apparently competently managed, and the tunnels they left are all mapped and are all very deep, between three hundred and a thousand feet deep below the surface. That mine stopped operating in the fifties, I believe, and by now, almost all the tunnels have likely filled with water or collapsed, but because they are so deep, nothing affects the surface. Another mine, the Blue Canyon Mine, was actually at the other end of this lake, but there have been no problems with that one, at least that I've heard about."

"It sounds like there is yet another mine that is more problematic."

"You got it—the Sehome Mine. It was owned by a San Francisco company and operated between 1853 and 1878. This mine operated under what is now downtown Bellingham. The problem is that all the mine maps and records were at the San Francisco company offices when San Francisco burned in 1906. Some of those tunnels must have been close to the surface because over the years some surface level subsidence—that's what they're called, rather than a sinkholes—has shown up on Bellingham streets and at least a couple of homes and garages have been affected. This latest one is the biggest and was enough to frighten folks all over town. Are their houses, their businesses, their kids' schools, their bank, or their favorite tavern going to be next? No one knows, and no one can offer any assurance that their worst fears won't be realized."

Maria yawned but noted, "It's only been two days, but already folks are saying that real estate prices have begun to crater. I'm sorry, guys, but I am fading fast. I think this pregnancy thing requires getting more rest than I am used to. I'll see you in the morning."

Alan and Luke had another beer and spent another hour reminiscing about their days as teammates on the Huntington Academy conference-winning base-ball team, about Luke's demoralizing second effort to pass the bar exam, and Alan's frustration of landing his dream job as a second engineering officer with the same cruise line as his wife worked for, only to have been put on the beach by the global pandemic. "But I do have some exciting news. Last week, I was accepted into a graduate program in marine engineering at the University of Tasmania."

"Tasmania! You're kidding, right?"

"Nope. They are one of only a few places in the world that offers an online program in my field. In fact, their marine studies division is world famous."

"What is their mascot, a Tasmanian devil?"

"Wrong again, smart ass. The mascot is actually 'Mumford the Lion.' Look it up."

"Al, really, that is quite impressive. Congratulations. How long will the program take to complete?"

"They have laid out a program for me that should take between eighteen and twenty-four months. I will then have as many college degrees as you do, buddy. But the real benefit will be that when this damn pandemic is over, I'll be even more attractive for chief engineering officer jobs than I currently am, though I know you might be asking, 'How could Alan be any more attractive?'"

"No, seriously, I get it and think you are making a very smart career move, but... the University of Tasmania?"

"You want another beer?"

"Alan, I am going to have to turn in too, if you don't mind. I have a nine a.m. meeting with a Bellingham Police lieutenant."

"No problem. I should retire too. As I told you, I have breakfast duty in the morning. I'll show you your room." He led Luke down the hall to a small but attractively furnished guest bedroom. "The bathroom is the next door down the hall. Don't worry about bothering us; we have quite an opulent bathroom suite in our room. Do you want me to wake you up at any particular time?"

"I have my watch alarm and was thinking about getting up around seven. I can quietly sneak out if that is too early for you guys."

"Nope. That will work. I'll have breakfast ready around seven-thirty. It is only a short drive into town and to the police department, so I'll see you at breakfast."

Luke shook Alan's hand and pulled him in for a hug. "God, it is good to see you and Maria. Thanks for taking in the pizza guy."

"Our pleasure."

Eight

At exactly 8:57 a.m., Luke and Sara Donovan pulled into the Bellingham Police Department parking lot in separate vehicles. Luke's rented sub-compact economy car looked like a toy next to her jacked-up, big tire, four-wheel-drive Ram truck. Luke unfolded his six-foot-four frame out of his car, put on his mask, and walked up behind the truck as Agent Donovan, who, at five foot two, literally had to jump out of the gas hog. Her mask had "DEA" boldly emblazoned across her face.

"Okay, I give up. Does DEA now issue monster trucks?"

"Hello to you, too, Agent Bitterman, and, no, this is not a standard issue DEA vehicle. It is what was left in the rental car inventory when I got in late last night, and they gave it to me for the same price as the one you have to peddle. I hope we don't have to put many miles on these vehicles on this assignment. I'm sure the green-eye-shade types will reject the gas bill I'd have to submit if we have to travel more than a few miles."

"Good to see you again, Sara. Shall we go in an find out what the good lieutenant has to show us?"

They had no sooner walked into the lobby when Lieutenant Tom Zale who had obviously been expecting them, walked up and elbow bumped both officers. "I'm a good enough detective to figure out that you're DEA Agent Donovan," pointing to Sara and her mask," which would make you Agent Bitterman of the Secret Service."

"And your name badge suggests you'd be Lieutenant Zale" replied Sara, with a smile hidden beneath her mask.

"Okay, now that we have established that we are all good at our jobs, let me show you what we have uncovered and who we think is behind it."

The three officers walked down the hall to Interrogation Room 2 as the lieutenant explained about the building collapse, the discovery of the items in Unit 2A, and the fingerprint revelation that said items belonged to one Roger Simpson, wanted fugitive. In the interrogation room, Tom pointed out the cash, the computers, the storage devices, the boxes of bank records, and picked up the mysterious note in a clear plastic evidence bag. "This is the most curious item," he said while handing it to Luke, who immediately handed it to Sara.

"She's the tech genius in this posse," Luke said.

"Oh, and here." Lieutenant Zale retrieved a folded document and handed it to Luke. "This is a signed search warrant. The judge thought these items, the disappearance of the individual, and his phony name were sufficient to sign off on us investigating all these items."

Sara immediately knew what the numbers were. "Well, I think I can confirm at least some of this pretty easily. This paper is often called a 'cheat sheet.' People just can't memorize all these long strings of numbers and letters. The longer strings are account or device identifiers, the shorter strings are probably personal signatures, and the list of words are 'seed' words, used to restore a lost, stolen, or damaged digital wallet. All this technical mumbo jumbo is part of a cryptocurrency operation. We'll have to figure out the phone numbers."

"You just said the magic word for me: 'cryptocurrency,'" Tom replied. "I know literally nothing about all that stuff. One of my younger officers apparently day-trades in them and tried to explain it all to me to no avail. I'm glad it's on your plate now, not mine. I'll leave you two to do your magic. If there's anything I can do to help, just give a holler. There's coffee down the hall in the work room."

"Lieutenant, there is one thing I know I will need. I see that the monitor on that desktop computer is broken. Do you happen to have a spare monitor that I could use?"

"Sure, back in a minute."

Luke looked at Sara and suggested, "How about I start on the paper trail and you see where the zeros and ones go."

"Makes sense to me. I'll race you to see who hits the finish line first."

"No way, Agent Donovan. Your part of the job is too simple, and mine is always complicated."

"Have you gotten immunized?"

"I'm shocked that you would ask such a personal question, but, yes, I have. How about you?"

"Yes, so let's just ditch these masks and stay at least six feet apart."

"You got it." They took off their masks and stuffed them into a pocket.

Tom returned with a monitor. Sara took it from him and connected it to the desktop computer.

Luke sat down at the end of a table, pulled out his laptop, and began to examine the bank records. The records were sorted by bank: two banks in Ferndale, one in Lynden, six in Bellingham, and two in Mount Vernon. The banks included every major large bank—Bank of America, Chase, Wells Fargo—but only one branch of each mega-bank. The rest were small community banks, including Shuksan Savings and Loan and Lynden Community Bank. Ten legitimate, unrelated banks, and all the accounts were personal checking accounts, not business accounts, and were opened about a year and half ago. He then chose one bank, Shuksan Savings and Loan, and examined the statements.

George Kennedy, as he was known to all the banks, made two or three, sometimes four, modest cash deposits into his account each month. Most months, the deposits totaled from $7,000 to $9,000. Shortly after each deposit, George used his debit card to make purchases of Bitcoins from the Freedom Exchange in amounts that were almost as large as his deposits.

Luke moved on to the records from George Kennedy's Bank of America account. They showed a similar pattern of deposits and expenditures. So did the records from the Chase Bank in Bellingham. Luke began to enter the monthly total deposits and expenditures from each bank into his own laptop spreadsheet.

Startled from his concentration, Luke heard Sara exclaim, "This guy is an idiot! The lieutenant said he had two deadbolt locks on his apartment, but neither of these computers are password protected. You turn it on and, voila, all is revealed! And he had a lot to hide."

"So, you are making progress?"

"Yep, but there is actually more here than we thought. I'll be able to tell you more in a while. Keep working, and we'll compare notes later."

"Hey, you were the one who interrupted me! I am going to get some coffee; do you want some?"

"No, thanks, this is quite stimulating enough." Sara laughed and redirected her efforts back to the screen.

Two and half hours later, Luke said, "I don't know about you, but I am getting hungry. Let's ask the lieutenant if there is a decent restaurant close by. My treat and I'll drive."

On the way back to the police station after a great lunch at Anthony's at Squalicum Harbor, Luke was a little confused. "I don't know what you're finding, but, so far, what I am seeing is that this George Kennedy—Roger Simpson—works really cheap. I am not done going through the bank records, but it looks like he deposits a bunch of cash and then quickly uses that cash to buy cryptocurrency for an amount just slightly less than he takes in. It appears about three percent less. He takes in a grand and then buys nine hundred and seventy dollars' worth of funny money. The records seem to suggest the total amount processed in this way is around ninety to a hundred thousand a month, which, if I am right about the three percent holdback, means he is doing all this driving around and making bank deposits and buying crypto for about twenty-eight hundred to three thousand a month. If the cash is coming from a drug network and he is exposed to serious criminal charges, that seems like a chump change return for his risk."

"I don't think the money laundering—or actually dirty money conversion into dirty crypto money—is his only business. What I am finding is that George or Roger, whatever, is running another business on the side. I'll know more by the end of the day."

Luke parked next to "the beast" and told Sara, "You go ahead. I have to make a phone call." Sara marched back into the police headquarters as if on a mission.

"Alan, this is Luke. I saw a barbeque on your deck. Would you mind if I picked up some steaks and brought a guest to dinner tonight?"

"If you bring steaks AND beer, that would be great."

"I'll see you guys around five-thirty, with steaks, beer, and the DEA agent I am working with. You might want to get your stash out of plain sight."

"Got it." They both laughed and hung up.

In the afternoon, Luke became preoccupied with the fact that George (Roger) had succeeded in making so many deposits without triggering any of the usual fire alarms that banks and the government had set up to detect money laundering. Under the Currency and Foreign Transaction Reporting Act of 1970, any deposit of over $10,000 required the bank to file a Form 8300 with the IRS. Moreover, banks that receive multiple smaller deposits to the same account that meet the $10,000 threshold are requested to file a "suspicious activity" report with the IRS.

Luke checked with the IRS and neither reports of deposits over $10,000 nor reports of suspicious activity had ever been filed on George's accounts. Somehow George must have had a credible story about his frequent cash deposits below the mandatory reporting limit. Luke left the interrogation room and sought out Lieutenant Zale.

"Say, Lieutenant, sorry to bother you, but do you have idea what George—Roger—did for a living?"

"I do, in fact. When I questioned his neighbors on Saturday, they said he was a professional gambler, and a good one."

"Thanks, Lieutenant, that's just what I needed to know."

It explained a lot. If a customer casually let it be known to tellers and others in banks where he did business and that he was a professional gambler, that would easily explain why he made frequent and rather large cash deposits. It would not necessarily be "suspicious activity." But casinos also had reporting requirements. They needed to report winnings above a certain level to the IRS. Luke knew that slot machine winnings of over $1,200 on a single pull precipitated an IRS filing and a poker tournament win over $5,000 did as well. He checked with the IRS, and no such filings had been made about payouts to a George Kennedy or a Roger Simpson in the last two years. That only left cash poker games as a possible source of unreported large cash winnings. Luke checked the websites of local casinos in Whatcom and Skagit counties and learned that, though they did have occasional poker tournaments, they did not have cash poker rooms. So, George (Roger) got a lot of cash and made deposits in ten different banks all below the mandatory reporting thresholds, with a legend of being a gambler. But he was likely not a gambler, as the absence of IRS reports of winnings demonstrated. Luke decided he would check with actual tellers at some of these banks on Tuesday to see if they volunteered their impression that George was simply a lucky local gambler.

Once Sara had recovered from her surprise that neither of George's computers was password protected, she had a productive day exploring George's files. He did not use either computer for much other than his illicit business. There were no emails to family, cooking recipes, porn, cute cat videos, airline boarding passes, nothing—just work related to the American Patriot Coin. A brief search of the computer's files uncovered a website for American Patriot Coin that announced:

> *Did you miss out on buying Amazon when it was $60 or Bitcoins when they were $70? Are you prepared for the inevitable coming collapse of the American dollar? Are you tired of high fees and transaction costs and long wait times for transaction confirmations incurred when dealing in Bitcoins? Are you willing to continue to be the victim of the Federal Reserve and Congress's manipulation of the dollar?*
>
> *Well, you can take control of your financial future and security with the soon-to-be offered American Patriot Coin. The AP Coin will be a 100% gold-backed alternative currency, supported by greatly improved blockchain technology, delivering fast, low cost, entirely secure transactions.*

Only eleven million AP Coins will be electronically minted. The AP Coin will be offered in an SEC-compliant Initial Coin Offering in late 2021.

The final technological refinements and legal work to develop the SEC-compliant ICO are well underway, but investors are now sought to bring AP Coins over the finish line. This is a tremendous opportunity for savvy investors. Purchase of AP Coin tokens during these final stages of development will allow investors to exchange each token for one AP Coin at the ICO price. Each AP Coin token is priced at $25. The AP Coin ICO price is expected to be $125, a 500% windfall for investors in AP Coin tokens! Only 32,000 tokens will be sold, and they are going fast, so do not wait!

"Luke, come look at this." Sara turned the screen so Luke could read what she had found. "This character is too smart for his own britches, but not smart enough. He obviously knows that, though the SEC has not declared cryptocurrencies to be a security, they have prosecuted several fraudulent ICOs as securities fraud. So, he's obviously decided that by selling 'tokens,' in what looks like a modestly legitimate crowd-funding exercise, he can evade SEC scrutiny, while still collecting money from 'investors' anxious to make a killing.

Underneath the pitch on the website is a 'Buy Now' section," Sara scrolled down the page, "that offers three ways for people to buy these tokens: credit card, PayPal, and Bitcoin transfers. No cash, check, or cashier's check options available."

"Can you tell how much he has collected?"

"Not from this, but I suspect one of the two digital wallets will show how much he has bilked people out of, and if we can get into his PayPal account, that might reveal more ill-gotten gains."

"So, it looks like Roger Simpson, aka George Kennedy, is involved in two enterprises—money laundering for someone else and conducting an internet scam on his own."

"It appears so. Let me get back into this. I'm sure I'll have more in a while."

An hour later, Luke left the interrogation room to get a cup of coffee, not asking Sara if she wanted any as she had declined his previous several offers. This time, however, Sara followed Luke down the hall.

"I'll give it to Simpson; he promoted his scam very cleverly. He sent hundreds of texts and emails to a variety of chat rooms, websites, and user groups with observations or questions about the American Patriot Coin, messages like, 'Hey, anyone out there see that offer about American Patriot Coins? It looks really tempting, is it real?' and 'My brother just turned me onto American Patriot Coins. Check it out!' When he sent these notes out all over the ether world, he used an anonymizer program to make it appear as if they all came from different people."

"Anonymizer program?" Luke asked as he poured himself a cup of coffee and lifted an empty cup toward Sara.

"Yes, please. Yeah, anonymizer programs delete the actual IP address of the computer generating the message to substitute it with another. Then the sender simply signs each message differently, like 'A. J.' or 'Sam' or 'W. Smith,' so it looks like dozens of people have sent messages from dozens of different computers, when all he has really done is create buzz... and business."

"Do you think anyone else is involved in this scam?"

"Nope, it looks like this is a one-man operation. It is also a limited-time scam. When people send in money, they get an email allegedly documenting the purchase of x number of certified AP Coin tokens. They have been told that the AP Coin ICO is scheduled to roll out in late 2021, so if the scam continued much longer, investors would start wanting specifics about the rollout and when they can exchange their tokens. Nope, this is a smash-and-grab exercise: collect the money, leave no forwarding address, and boogey."

Walking back to the interrogation room, Luke asked Sara, "Hey, tonight I am going to stop and pick up some steaks and beer and head out to Lake Whatcom where I am staying with a couple of friends. Would you like to join us for dinner? I checked with them, and they said they would love to have you join us."

"Luke, that is awfully nice of you—and them. I would love to. The thing I hate most about being on the road for these kinds of assignments is eating dinner alone in some restaurant a motel clerk or cabbie swears is the best place in town, only to discover it is not."

Luke and Sara went back to work.

At 5:15, Luke announced that he was done for the day and Sara stood up and stretched her whole five-foot-two frame. "Just give me one more minute; there is something I want to check".

"Sure, is there something I could help with?"

"No," Sara opened her laptop, "I just want to see how much money is associated with these damn wallets. Actually, would you read me the long identifier from that cheat sheet?" Luke read out the first string of numbers and letters. "Eureka! That wallet has about twenty grand worth of Bitcoin in it, and it has had several transactions with another wallet that matches the second string of numbers on the cheat sheet. The second wallet, the destination wallet for the transfers from the first wallet, has almost two million dollars' worth of Bitcoin! Read me the identifier string for that other wallet, the one with the signature and seed words."

Luke read the numbers, and once again, Sara let out a hoot. "This one has around a hundred and fifty thousand worth of Bitcoin in it."

"How'd you do that?"

"It is simple, really, and a weakness of the whole cryptocurrency technology. When someone offers a crypto, they must assure purchasers that any given coin can only be spent once at a time, like a dollar. If you have a greenback, you can only spend it once, and then the person who received it can only spend it once. Possession of the piece of paper ensures that the same dollar can't be spent more than once by the same person. In crypto world, the way they guarantee this non-reproducibility is that every transaction is recorded on a distributed public ledger. That is, you can look up and see if a purchaser, for example, has enough crypto to purchase the item you are selling, and then if the transaction is completed, it all shows up on the public ledger, which must, of course, be 'public.' I just typed in the account identifier and was able to see that wallet one has twenty K, wallet two has two million, and wallet one has transferred Bitcoins many times to wallet two . Clearly, Roger Simpson is taking in cash, depositing it in small amounts in numerous banks, buying Bitcoins for his wallet, and then transferring a lot of Bitcoin to someone else, who has at least two million. Money laundering and, most likely, drugs. But enough of this. I am tired and hungry. Let's go buy some steaks and beer and resume this exploration tomorrow morning."

"Good plan, but I think I'd better call the US Attorney's Office and let them know what we suspect." Luke made a brief call and followed DEA Agent Sara Donovan out the door. "Why don't you follow me in the beast. I'll be stopping at the grocery store, and we can convoy out to my friends' place."

Sara gave him a thumbs up.

They didn't see Lieutenant Zale on the way out but left word with the desk sergeant that they would be back the next morning around 8:30.

***

The evening at the Washington's was a delight for all. During the pandemic, the Washingtons had had so few chances to relax and just chat with others over the last year that they reveled in the opportunity. Sara let her hair down as if the four of them had been fast friends for years. Luke took pleasure in talking with people he genuinely liked and about something other than work.

After Alan, Luke, and Sara had finished their beers and Maria her lemonade, Alan asked, "Another round?"

Sara said, "Thanks," and handed her empty to Alan.

Maria handed her empty glass to Alan and nodded. Following Alan, Luke took his own empty into the kitchen and told his best friend, "I need to check in with Annie." He pulled out his phone and retreated to the front hallway for some privacy.

"Hi, love, how ya—"

Annie interrupted, "Luke, you missed it! Today, Ashley graduated from her tummy scooting to crawling. Well, not exactly crawling yet, but she got up on her hands and knees and tried to figure out the coordination to motor across the floor. She landed on her nose a few times but must have thought it was fun because I've never seen her laugh so much. It was so darn cute!"

"And I thought I might be the one with news tonight! I am so sorry to have missed that! Did she ever figure out the coordination and make tracks?"

"Nope, but I think she was actually motivated by playing with Ricky yesterday, and I'll bet she figures it out tomorrow or the next day. She is a fast learner. I assume you'll be home in time to see this."

"Not clear yet when I'll be heading home. I know we'll be busy tomorrow, but maybe the next day. I'll let you know. I am here at Alan and Maria's for dinner tonight." He deliberately didn't mention Sara, not because of any impropriety but he simply didn't want to cause any unwarranted concerns. "They both send you their love."

"Say 'hi' for me. I wish I were there to be catching up with them, but I am glad I was here today. It was so exciting."

"I'll bet you won't be so excited about little miss's mobility when in a week or two, you turn around and find that she has motored off to parts unknown."

"That's why we have to have two sets of eyes to keep track of her. Get home as soon as you can."

"I will, hon. I will call again tomorrow. Don't you dare jump the gun and teach her to walk before I get there."

"Good night, Luke. Talk with you tomorrow."

Luke returned to the living room just as Alan was going out on the deck to fire up the barbeque and put on the rib eye steaks Luke had brought. "Anything I can help with?"

"Nope, got it handled. Maria and Sara are making a salad and chattering like long-lost friends. She seems to be a really nice person and a tough cop."

"Oh yeah, she is both. Like me, she came to law enforcement somewhat circuitously."

"Did she go to law school too?"

"No, she graduated from Portland State with a double major in computer science and management information systems. After graduation, she joined the Multnomah County Sheriff's Office as a civilian employee in their IT department, where she distinguished herself and became interested in becoming a sworn officer. A captain there championed her case and, long story short, she worked as a deputy sheriff in the narcotics division for about three years, when she applied to and was accepted as a DEA agent. She works out of the Portland DEA office. She's a veritable genius when it comes to IT stuff, but don't be fooled by her height. She is also an award-winning amateur weightlifter. So, yes, nice, smart, and tough."

"Sounds like she could kick your ass."

"I wouldn't want to test that."

"By the way, I told you yesterday that folks in Bellingham are freaking out over the coal tunnels and building collapse. Today, in the letters to the editor, one woman wrote about how this was just the beginning of the end times and all should prepare. Another genius wanted to find out how to sue the real estate or title companies for not revealing that his house sat on top of collapsing mine tunnels. The paper also had an article about a guy who was going around and telling people he could, for a hefty fee, probe the ground under their houses to determine whether they are sitting on top of an impending disaster. He showed potential customers a machine that turned out to be a power washer with a mower blade housing mounted on the bottom. It would be funny except for the fact that dozens of people fell for it and paid him."

After dinner, Luke and Alan cleared the dishes and cleaned up the kitchen. Maria and Sara chatted about a shared following of women's soccer. When the men joined the women, the conversation turned to Alan and Maria's prospects of returning to sea and the likelihood the cruise industry could return to pre-pandemic growth. No one knew, but Alan sounded optimistic.

Luke walked Sara to the elevator and told her he would see her in the interrogation-evidence room around 8:30.

Nine

Tuesday morning, Luke pulled into the parking lot at the police station at 8:15. The beast was already parked there.

When he walked into Interrogation Room 2, Luke observed, "Well, you're the early bird this morning. How long have you been here?"

"I woke up early and with nothing else to do, so I decided to get to it. I've been here about an hour, but I have unearthed a little more of our puzzle."

"Oh yeah? What would that be?"

"A couple of things, actually. First, I checked into those wallet accounts again this morning and guess what? They have both been emptied. Yesterday, the one had around twenty K in Bitcoin and the other, around a hundred and fifty K in Bitcoin. This morning, both have been wiped clean. That means that Roger has gotten two new wallets and, using the seed words from that cheat sheet, established the new wallets and transferred all the assets from these old wallets to the new ones. He must have a duplicate of the cheat sheet on him."

"Okay, so he is out there and, at least as far as the assets being under his control, is back in business. Interesting."

"Not only that. I had assumed, or hoped, that those numbers on the sheet were for cell phones. My cell phone identification and location app not only proved they are cell phone numbers, it gave me the listed owner of each phone and an approximate location using the cell phones' own GPS capability."

"I must admit, I didn't know there was such technology. Is that app standard issue at DEA?"

"No this is my own personal subscription." Luke was not surprised. "Can anyone get it?"

"Oh yeah. Anyone can get an app on their phone to identify and trace a cell phone. Let me show you." She pulled out her phone and asked, "What is your cell phone number?" Luke told her his number, and she thumbed the digits into her phone. "Okay, this says that the owner of the phone with that number is Lucas Bitterman, and here's your address." She showed Luke the phone.

"Yep, that's my home address."

"But look here. It also shows that that phone is currently right here."

"You say anyone can get that app on their phone?"

"Yep, the free version only gives the phone's owner's name. For the address and location, you have to pay a fee, but it is readily available."

"So, what did you find out about the phone numbers on the cheat sheet?"

"The 916 number belongs to a Samuel Parker in the Sacramento area, and the 360 number belongs to one Steven Schmidt here in Bellingham. The first phone is physically in Sacramento, and the second one is right here in town. I would suggest that we split them up and find out what we can about Parker and Schmidt. How about I take Parker and you take Schmidt?"

"You got it." Luke sat down and opened his laptop, but even before he turned it on, he left the room to get a cup of coffee.

***

Tuesday morning, George checked out his motel and tossed his new laptop computer, briefcase, and hardware digital wallets in the back seat of his Mustang. His enforced isolation in the Mount Vernon motel had been productive. He'd taken his two new wallets and installed the seed words for each, duplicating the two wallets left behind in the condo. He had swept the balances from the orphaned wallets into his new wallets. Now, even if someone came into possession of the original wallets, they would be empty. The only thing left to do before hitting the road was to retrieve his gold.

George left the motel parking lot and took the entrance for I-5 north for the thirty-eight-mile trip through Bellingham to Ferndale, planning to arrive shortly after the nine-a.m. opening of the bank. He stayed in the right lane and kept his speed five miles an hour under the posted speed limit. He was more than a little apprehensive about returning to Bellingham, but he just could not imagine leaving the area without his gold; it was a large percentage of what he had collected so far in his sale of AP Coin tokens.

In less than an hour, George pulled into the parking lot of Shuksan Savings and Loan. He double checked his phone for the actual number of his safety deposit box and the name of the cute teller he had most dealt with, then fingered the box key on his key chain. He grabbed the empty briefcase he had bought in Mount Vernon.

No one was in line, so George went to his familiar teller. "Hi, there, Gwen, how are you today?"

"Just fine, George, and you? Are the cards still running your way?"

"A bit of a cool spell lately, so I don't have a deposit, but I do need to get into my safety deposit box."

"Sure, no problem. I'll meet you at the end counter." The teller signed out of her computer and met George to begin the sign-in process for access to safety deposit boxes. After that, they entered the safe, each inserted their key, and George withdrew his box.

"Do you need to go into one of the security rooms, George?" she asked.

"Yeah, but it won't take but a minute."

When George closed the door, he opened the safety deposit box, withdrew seventy-two gold bullion coins, and placed them in his briefcase. He feared turning in his empty box might attract attention, so he left the security booth and signaled Gwen he was done. When the teller returned the empty box to its rightful slot in the safe, George said, "Thanks, Gwen, I'll see you next time."

"Good luck, George."

George had to force himself to walk slowly back to his car before he headed back south for any destination other than Bellingham.

***

Washington State Patrol Officer Duane Philips had just finished meeting with a fellow officer for a brief coffee break. He got in his white patrol car, checked that all the computers and other electronics were up and green lighted, and headed for the Sunset Avenue entrance to I-5. Heading south, he noted that the traffic was remarkably light for a Tuesday morning and concluded that maybe some people had taken the day off from work to make a four-day holiday. Whatever the reason, he was pleased to see little traffic.

Only minutes after turning onto I-5 and just past the Lakeway exit, the computer chimed a hit on the automated, forward-looking license plate scanning video system. He looked at the computer screen and was informed that the license that triggered the alarm belonged to a fugitive with an outstanding felony warrant and a suspect in a money-laundering and drug-distribution investigation. The vehicle described in the BOLO matched the black Mustang in front of him. He called for any law enforcement assistance that was in the vicinity and continued to follow the Mustang at a distance.

Only minutes after placing the call for assistance, Officer Philips saw a Bellingham Police black and white enter the freeway and pull up behind the WSP cruiser. Officer Philips pulled up closer to the Mustang, turned on his lights, and followed the slowing Mustang to the shoulder of the highway. The police cruiser pulled past the WSP unit and the Mustang and pulled onto the shoulder directly in front of the Mustang.

George was in a panic: Why were the police pulling him over? He had not been speeding. Did the cops already have a search out for him because of the equipment and money in the condo? Could it be the expired tags on the Washington license plate he had stolen? He hoped to God it was the tags.

Officer Philips put on his smokey bear hat and approached the vehicle, with his hand on his holster. One of the Bellingham police officers approached the vehicle on the passenger side. George rolled down his window. "Officer, what's the problem? I know I wasn't speeding."

"Could I ask you to keep your hands on the wheel, sir, and with one hand show me some identification." George pulled out his wallet and handed the officer his somewhat valid Washington State driver's license in the name of George Kennedy.

Officer Philips looked at the license and asked, "Is the information on this license current and correct, sir?" George nodded. "I am going to ask you to wait here for a few minutes." Philips took the driver's license back to his unit, signaling to the police officer to keep an eye on the driver.

After what seemed to George an eternity, Officer Philips returned to the driver's side window and asked George to step out of the car.

"What the hell? I didn't do anything. What are you hassling me for?"

The WSP officer turned George around and told him to place his hands on the top of the car. He took George's right hand and closed a handcuff on his wrist, then took George's left arm behind his back and hooked up the other side of the cuffs. "Mr. Simpson, you are under arrest pursuant to an outstanding bench warrant in Sacramento and for suspicion of presenting a false identity to a police officer." Philips opened the rear door of his cruiser and directed George into the rear seat and solidly closed the door.

WSP Officer Philips waved to the Bellingham police officers. "Thanks for the backup guys. I appreciate it. Could you arrange to have this vehicle towed to the impound yard?"

It took only minutes to drive to the Whatcom County Jail on Grand Avenue and get George checked into a holding cell.

George fumed, mumbling, "Shit!" He hoped that because the officer called him 'Mr. Simpson,' his arrest was only related to the identity charge waiting for him in Sacramento and not to his money laundering or phony coin offering in Bellingham. George assumed that his car would be searched at the impound yard, and they were going to have questions about him carrying around about five pounds of gold and maybe about his computer and digital wallets too. In that case, there would be no way he could possibly talk his way out of this mess.

He kicked the lidless metal toilet as hard as he could out of frustration, which not only hurt his foot, but drew a visit from the guard, who told him, "Cool your jets, fella. Yes, you are in a world of hurt, but taking it out on the accommodations won't help."

Ten

At 11:45 a.m., Tom walked into Interrogation Room 2 and announced to Luke and Sara, "We got him. The WSP just picked up Roger Simpson on I-5 heading south. He was taken into custody and is currently in the county jail on the bench warrant. I talked with the assistant US attorney, and she would like to meet with me and you two at one o'clock in my office."

Luke smiled at Sara and turned to Tom. "Good news, Lieutenant, we'll be there."

Luke returned to his search on Steven Schmidt and told Sara. "I think I'll just work through lunch so we can have as much as possible to tell the AUSA."

"I agree." Sara went back to chasing down the information on Samuel Parker.

By 12:15, Sara thought she had unearthed all that was available on Samuel Parker and, without mentioning anything to Luke, began to look more deeply into Samuel Parker's phone records. After a half an hour, she shared with Luke that she had discovered a pattern in the phone calls that needed examining. "Turns out that Samuel Parker phones two 619 numbers in the San Diego area: one is listed as belonging to Harold Parker and the other to an Arturo Cruz. Samuel phoned each at least five or six times a month."

"Sara, you do recall that there is a Fourth Amendment, right?"

"No worry, I didn't get into any of the content of the calls, just the fact that the numbers had been called. I think you legal types call it the 'third-party doctrine.'"

"That's right. So, I assume it's not a coincidence to have one Parker phoning another Parker. Father? Brother?"

"Don't know yet, but the other number might be more interesting. It is listed as belonging to Arturo Cruz. Mr. Cruz has a California driver's license with an address in National City. Two and a half years ago, he was arrested on a major felony drug charge—in possession of more than four hundred grams of heroin, several firearms, and a large quantity of cash. Two others were also arrested at the same time. Cruz went to trial, and all charges were dismissed on a motion to suppress all the evidence discovered in the apartment. The arrest report read like an open-and-shut case, a by-the-book arrest and seizure, so I went to the transcript of the trial and was more than a little surprised to see that the motion to dismiss was sophomoric and had little or no legal basis to be granted—but you would know more about the legal viability of the motion than I do. In short, he walked because of a genuinely incompetent or corrupt judge; no rational judge would have granted the dismissal. The judge was a guy named Harold Parker. He's been on the bench for about twenty years and is probably close to retirement. No judicial complaints against him, other than a couple of snarky reports of him falling asleep during a trial. Couldn't find anything about current employment for Cruz."

"So, Samuel Parker routinely phones his father, Harold Parker, and Arturo Cruz, a drug dealer who benefited from a questionable dismissal motion by the father?"

"Yeah."

"Well, there is more. Samuel Parker's driver's license confirms an address in a tony suburb of Sacramento called Granite Bay. I did a Google Street View drive-by, and his digs are upper end, amazing for a guy who makes his living as a public defender. No record. But guess what? Parker was Roger Simpson's public defender when Roger scooted out of town and failed to appear at his identify theft trial."

"That would explain why Simpson had his phone number.... Parker was his lawyer, but why would he store the number on the cheat sheet rather than on his phone?"

"Good question."

"Maybe we can get answers to those questions after we meet with the AUSA, and I can tell you about Steven Schmidt."

***

Luke and Sara walked down the hall to the lieutenant's office. The door was open, and Tom signaled for them to come in and sit down. An attractive tall forty-something woman was sitting opposite the lieutenant and rose and turned to Sara and Luke.

"Hello, my name is Melody Eniss," she said as she reached out to shake hands with the two. "I am an assistant US attorney for the Western District of Washington, and I assume you are the two federal agents who have been digging into this Simpson case."

Luke and Sara each introduced themselves. Luke added, "We chatted briefly on the phone the other day, Ms. Ennis."

"We did and I appreciate being notified early in a case like this. And, please, call me Mel."

Tom, who seemed to have known Mel before today, invited Mel, Sara, and Luke to take a seat. He turned to Sara and Luke, "Please give us the CliffNotes' version of what you have unearthed about Roger Simpson's activities."

Even the short version of facts took the two federal agents more than forty minutes to explain. Neither Mel or Tom interrupted their recitation. Luke and Sara were very precise in differentiating what they knew, what they suspected, and what lines of inquiry were ahead of them. When they had exhausted their report and sat back in their chairs, Mel summarized the situation.

"So, we have a person passing himself as George Kennedy, who was out of his condo when the building crumbled. When he returned to the broken building, he attempted, unsuccessfully, to get some valuables from his condo, saw too many police around, and took off. The money, bank records, computer files, and digital wallets all suggest money laundering, but there were no drugs or guns found in the unit, so drug trafficking at this point is conjecture. The money-laundering operation appears to process eighty to hundred grand a month, buying crypto currency and then transferring the crypto onto another unidentified party. The phony cryptocurrency selling scheme Mr. Simpson was running seemed to be about in mid-scam when you uncovered it. He had taken in a lot of money but was still offering it for sale, so he wasn't done yet—but the evidence is overwhelming. Transactions on the two digital wallets prove he was active in those accounts after he left town and had replaced the lost wallets."

The lieutenant's phone rang and he listened for about thirty seconds. "Sorry, for the interruption, but I just learned that when we checked Simpson's car into the impound yard, approximately five pounds of gold coins—worth around a hundred and fifty thousand dollars—was discovered in a briefcase found on the back seat of the car. There were also two digital wallets in the car."

"Interesting," Melody Ennis said almost under her breath. More forcefully, she continued, "So, it sounds like this Simpson was a launderer of other people's dirty money, but we can't prove it is dirty because we have no evidence of drugs. The bank records show clear evidence of structuring. Then, ever the entrepreneur, he set out on his own and was running a phony crypto scam, from which he has already scored a lot of money in his personal digital wallet and a few pounds of gold coins. Both enterprises involve wire fraud and, possibly, mail fraud. He also has a date in Sacramento on the identify theft charge, and I'll bet the SEC and the IRS would have some questions for our busy Mr. Simpson. Here's the problem I have: Simpson is just a low-level dupe with aspirations of becoming a big-time scammer. What I really want are the drugs and dealers that produced the cash he processed and the higher ups who are making all the real money and running this operation. In short, I am hoping that we could get Roger Simpson to help us swim downstream and sweep up drugs and dealers and help us swim upstream to get the Mr. or Ms. Big. Any problem with that approach?"

Luke shook his head, and Sara said, "Not here."

Tom asked, "So should we go see Mr. Simpson?"

Eleven

At noon on Tuesday, Arturo Cruz and his brother-in-law, Manny Cortes, walked down the ramp onto the pier of Hanson's Marina on Shelter Island in San Diego Bay. The harbor was the base for many deep-sea fishing charter boats. Arturo and Manny had made this trip three times before, once about every six months. They walked out the dock until they stood next to the *Sunny Daze*, a thirty-six-foot Hatteras sportfish cruiser.

The skipper called out, "Howdy, fellas, come aboard. Looks like we'll be in for some good fishing."

Manny stepped onto the aft deck of the fishing boat, and Arturo handed over two large duffel bags and jumped on board himself.

"Grab yourselves a beer if you like, while I get us underway and on our way south."

Manny grabbed two beers from the cooler and handed one to Arturo, then they both sat down in the comfortable deck chairs to enjoy the view on the way out of San Diego Bay, past Point Loma, and south past the Coronado Islands, just off Tijuana. When the sun had begun to set and there was nothing but empty black Pacific Ocean to look at, Manny and Arturo went into the spacious cabin. Manny went to the bottles of liquor in the latched cupboard in the galley.

"Don't you be hitting the hard stuff too much tonight. We'll have to be on our toes."

"Don't you worry about me, Art. First, I hold my liquor well, better than you, and second, we have the routine down; we haven't had any trouble before, have we?"

"No, but just the same, not too much, okay?"

The captain of the *Sunny Daze* climbed down from the bridge and sat with Manny and Arturo. "So, is it the same coordinates and times as in the past?"

Arturo nodded.

"I hate to tell you this, guys, but this will be the last trip at our old price. Next time, this trip will run forty grand. I am just running a lot of risk here. If we got caught, I'd lose my boat and my business. I'd be up shit creek. I am willing to run that risk, but not anymore for twenty-five K. The new price is firm."

Arturo smiled. He had expected this and had guessed that the skipper would go for $50,000 a trip, so $40,000 was still a reasonable price. "Skipper, you took the words right out of my mouth. I was going to talk to you about giving you a raise, so, sure, no problem. Just keep getting us to our rendezvous and home in one piece with our product, and you will continue to enjoy this gravy train. By the way, if we were actual fishermen, what would you be charging for this day-and-half cruise?"

"About two grand, depending how many guys and how much beer they drink."

"So, our charter is the best gig you ever get?"

"Yes, but it is also the scariest. Drunken boors who think they can fish are a lot easier to handle than the Mexican Navy or some Coast Guard cutter, if they decided to get nosy."

"Don't worry, bro. We've got this thing down."

At 1:45 a.m., the *Sunny Daze* was precisely at the GPS coordinates for the meeting and drifting slowly nine miles off the Mexican coast. At two a.m., an unlighted twenty-six-foot-long panga could be heard but not seen heading toward the *Sunny Daze*. The panga cut its 150-horsepower outboard motor and drifted to the side of the sportfisher. Four men in the panga quickly offloaded eleven hundred pounds of heroin, packaged in one-kilo plastic-wrapped bricks: ten bricks to a box, making fifty boxes to be handed on board the *Sunny Daze*. Once the shipment had been transferred, Arturo tossed the larger of his two duffle bags to the crew of the panga, and the delivery boat fired up its engine and headed back toward shore. Not a word had been spoken between the panga crew and Arturo or Manny. Before the sound of the departing panga faded away, the skipper of the *Sunny Daze* fired up his engines for the return trip to San Diego, and Arturo and his brother-in-law began packing the fifty boxes in a compartment specially constructed beneath the bed in the forward berth. Not that secreting the drugs in their hiding place would do any good against a drug-sniffing dog, but it would likely be successful if someone boarded the boat believing that the passengers were, in fact, really fishermen. That was the prime task for the next ten or so hours—to catch fish and drink.

When Arturo had been arrested, he and his partners had believed that conducting criminal activity late at night, in the darkest corners, and in the seediest part of town was the strategy to avoid detection. His arrest and interrogation had revealed that that was precisely when and where law enforcement expected illegal activity to be conducted and where and when they were the most ubiquitous and vigilant. He stored that lesson away for future use, and when he had been sprung on a technicality, he put into practice an alternative approach to crime. His new strategy was reinforced when he wandered around the neighborhoods surrounding two of the local colleges and marveled at how openly the young white dealers shopped their wares—and no one seemed to give them any notice.

Arturo concluded that the issue was not about not being seen, but more about not being suspected or attracting any attention. The robber who walked away from a robbery had a better chance of getting away than did the fool who ran. The shooter who wore a suit and melted with the other suits in a restaurant had a better chance of avoiding apprehension than did the shooter who wore camo and a balaclava. The application of this criminal strategy in the current operation was simple: be on a recognized and respectable fishing charter boat and appear to be fishermen enjoying a two-day charter and catching fish. Hell, the Coast Guard might just come along side and say, "Hey, have you guys seen a fast speed boat carrying men with automatic weapons and a half ton of drugs?"

At first light, Arturo and Manny began to fish in earnest. They caught bottom fish, a few tuna, and one sail fish. They cleaned the fish sloppily, being sure to leave a lot of fish blood and guts on the deck. They packed the fish fillets in ice and stored the boxes in two large coolers on the back deck of the boat. The skipper trolled slowly, obviously not in any hurry to get anywhere. Just outside of San Diego harbor, Arturo and Manny put away the fishing gear and sat on deck, once again drinking beer. Arturo sat and watched the boat traffic entering and leaving San Diego Bay and, once again, ran the numbers mentally.

Eleven hundred pounds of heroin, at 453 grams per pound, was 498,300 'dime bags,' which, at around $15 per bag, was about $7,500,000. And this was their fourth trip south, so, with this shipment, they would have brought in around $30 million. Sure beat actual work.

A Coast Guard cutter was leaving the harbor just as the *Sunny Daze* passed the submarine base on Point

Loma. No one aboard the cutter appeared to pay any attention to the *Sunny Daze*. The skipper docked his boat, and Manny and Arturo went to the head of the pier to pick up a couple of large push carts that boaters used to haul groceries, fish, personal items, and, in this case, drugs to and from vehicles and their boats. Manny loaded four of the heroin boxes in the bottom of one cart and topped it with two boxes of fresh fish fillets. Arturo did the same. Arturo went first, then five minutes later, Manny followed. Both unloaded their carts into a large utility van with "AAA Plumbing" boldly painted on the side. Each returned to the boat and sat and had a beer for another ten minutes before making another run up the dock—no need to be seen making many non-stop runs up the dock, which might attract attention.

It took almost two hours for Manny and Arturo to transfer all their shipment to the plumbing truck. Before Arturo's last trip up the dock to the van, he handed the skipper the last of the duffle bags he brought aboard and said, "Thanks, Skipper, another good trip. We'll see you in about six months and, yes, the next duffel bag will be a little heavier. Thanks again." Then he walked slowly to the van, got in, drove home, and parked in the garage.

Manny said, "Hey, bro, can I take some of that fish home?"

"Some? You can have all of it. I hate fish."

Manny piled two boxes on top of each other, hoisted them for the three-block walk to his home, and told Arturo that he couldn't take all of it.

Twelve

Mel, Luke, and Sara walked into the interrogation room in the Whatcom County Jail. Roger Simpson had been brought from his cell and was sitting in a chair with his handcuffed wrists resting on a table. Tom was in the viewing room adjacent to the interrogation room. Luke was surprised by Roger Simpson's countenance. He did not adopt the insolent visage so many arrestees do: he did not appear frightened nor looked confused, as most do. He simply looked tired and distressed.

Mel pulled out the only other chair in the room and sat down. "Mr. Simpson, I am Melody Ennis, Assistant US Attorney for the Western District of Washington. He," she pointed to Luke," is Special Agent Bitterman of the Secret Service, and she," she nodded in Sara's direction, "is Special Agent Donovan of the DEA.

You were read your rights when you were arrested. Do you now wish to assert your right to an attorney being present for this discussion?"

Roger Simpson simply shook his head no.

"Well, then, I would like you to sign this piece of paper that says you have declined to have an attorney present during our conversation." She scooted the paper and pen across the table, and Roger signed it without a word.

"Okay, Mr. Simpson, I have some good news and some bad news. The good news is that the police were able to save your valuables from your collapsed condo building. The bad news is the police were able to save your valuables from your collapsed condo building. We don't need to tell you all the evidence of all your criminal activity that we have; you already know what you did and what you left behind. What you may not know is that these two agents have spent the better part of two days finding more information than you might think they could have unearthed. What it all adds up to, Mr. Simpson, is that you are going to be arraigned for a large variety of crimes: money laundering, structuring..."

Roger raised his eyebrows.

"You didn't go to law school did you, Mr. Simpson?" Mel asked.

Roger looked at her like she had grown two heads.

"I thought not, so I will tell you. Structuring is defined in Section 5324, Title 31 US Code as making deposits into banks for the purpose of evading the bank reporting requirements under the Currency and Foreign Transaction Reporting Act of 1970. Structuring itself is a felony and subject to considerable prison time. Your bank records are slam-dunk proof of structuring. So, returning to the list of your crimes: money laundering, structuring, probably drug trafficking, but we are still working on that one, wire fraud related to your cryptocurrency token scam, and that will likely lead to mail fraud as well. Then, there is the identity theft and failure to appear charges you will be revisiting in Sacramento. All told, I would say you are looking at a minimum of forty years in prison, and that's before the SEC and the IRS have a conversation with you about the securities law violations in your initial coin, or token, offering and the fact that you appear to have not filed any tax returns for, well, forever. Oh, and by the way, George Kennedy would like his name and social security number back. That really wasn't very bright, Mr. Simpson, to use the identity of one of your identify-theft victims." Melody Ennis turned to Luke and Sara. "Have I left anything out?"

Luke replied for both, "Only a couple of minor charges that would probably only add another eighteen months to his sentence."

Mel continued, "Now, Mr. Simpson, I seem to have been doing all the talking. Do you have anything you'd like to say?"

Roger was seriously beginning to question whether simply clamming up was the best strategy. Maybe he should have demanded an attorney present, but the last time he did that, the attorney encouraged him to skip bail, leave town, and start the money-laundering business. He could not decide how best to proceed, so he stuck to his silence strategy.

"Well, Mr. Simpson. I have a few more things to say. Actually, it is a question that you would be wise to consider answering. I don't think you are really a bad guy; I know because I deal with really bad guys every day. I think you had very few career choices that appealed to you and some reasonable computer skills, so you fell into a couple of jobs that happened to be illegal. Now, I suspect the people who are out there on the street selling drugs and killing people are the bad guys. I also suspect that the person or persons to whom you send money—or Bitcoins—every month are also bad people and getting terribly rich while you sit up here in the rain and simply move money around for what appears to be modest rewards. I really want to stop the bad guys you are dealing with, and so I am going to make you an offer, an offer that will only be available until I leave this room. If you cooperate with these investigators and help us stop these bad guys and if you cooperate in unraveling your AP Coin fraud scheme, I can make some or most of the charges we discussed disappear, and for the ones we can't disappear, I will be willing to recommend to the judge the minimum sentence the law will allow. Let me be clear, if you do not cooperate, I will pursue all these charges and more... and you will be sent away for most of the rest of your life. If you take this one-time offer, you are likely to serve only two or three years at the most. Do you understand this offer Mr. Simpson?"

Roger's mind was racing. On the one hand, he was familiar with the old saying that if an offer appeared to be too good to be true, it probably was. On the other hand, he had always heard that one should not look a gift horse in the mouth. Roger spoke for the first time to the three in the room, "Yes, I understand the offer, but I would have to see it in writing and signed by you or a judge or somebody so that it can be enforced if I agree to cooperate."

"Mr. Simpson, that is a perfectly reasonable request." She reached into her briefcase and pulled out a two-page, typed document. "This, Mr. Simpson, is the document I drafted reflecting what we have been talking about. It says, in necessary legal language, that if, and only if, you completely and fully cooperate in the investigations we have discussed and if you cooperate in unraveling your crypto coin scam—all to our satisfaction—we will decline to prosecute you for your part in these crimes." She handed the document to Roger, who spent the next five minutes reading and re-reading it and trying to understand all the legal mumbo-jumbo.

It slowly dawned on Roger that the document appeared to do just what the lady prosecutor said it did and was a cheap way out of his huge mess. "Okay. I'll sign it."

"Remember, Mr. Simpson, you also have to live up to the terms of this agreement to fully and completely cooperate. Any effort to not be fully forthcoming will result in an abrogation of the agreement and we will proceed with numerous prosecutions."

"I get it, lady. Just give me a pen and let me get back to my cell in time for dinner. I'll start talking and singing like a bird tomorrow." Roger signed the document and handed it back to Mel, who put it in her briefcase.

Luke, Sara, and Mel left the interrogation room and chatted briefly in the hallway. Tom joined them. Mel proposed, "Tomorrow morning, I would like you two to begin debriefing Mr. Simpson. You know all the holes in our understanding about what is going on here and what he can fill in. Go slowly and record the sessions. It may take a few days of inquiry to get everything he knows or doesn't know he knows, but it might just lead us both up- and downstream and wrap this operation up."

On the walk back to the police station, Tom and Mel walked ahead and chatted; Luke and Sara followed behind. Luke asked Sara if she would like to join him and the Washingtons for dinner again. "No, thanks. I think I am going to spend a little more time with the, now, four digital wallets to prepare for tomorrow, grab some dinner at an Italian joint I saw near my motel, and then tuck in with one of those huge Ken Follett books I picked up at Sea-Tac while I was waiting for my connection. You go ahead, though, and say 'hi and thanks' to Alan and Maria."

"Will do. See you tomorrow around eight a.m. for the walk over to the jail?"

"Sounds good."

***

After dinner at the Washington's lakeview condo, Luke called Annie and then Neal Hanson, his boss. Ashley was reported to still be getting up on all fours—her hands and knees—and occasionally making a few tentative feet before she fell on her nose and tummy and, again, laughed at the hilarity of the whole process. Annie reported Ashley did make some progress a couple of times—backwards. Luke was disappointed to have to tell Annie that he was going to be in Bellingham for a couple more days. Ever the supportive wife, Annie tried and failed to respond that the extended absence of her husband was okay: "Just come home as soon as you can."

"Hi, Neal, sorry to bother you so late," Luke said, but he knew that Neal had answered his phone in the bar at his favorite after-work stop. Neal was divorced and had lost many of his friends and acquaintances in the process. He lived in a small utilitarian apartment and was, if he were honest with himself, quite lonely. "No problem, Luke, how's it going up there in rainy country?"

"Pretty well actually, but it is taking a little longer than I, or Annie, had hoped. Sara and I retrieved a whole truckload of evidence of money laundering, probable drug trafficking, wire and mail fraud, securities violations, and several other crimes, and the locals arrested the main guy involved so far. The assistant US attorney confronted the fellow with the likelihood of an exceedingly long prison term for his various activities, and he has agreed to cooperate, in exchange for a 'decline to prosecute' agreement. Agent Donovan and I will start the in-depth interviews with the person arrested tomorrow. My guess is that this will take another couple of days, but if the bird really sings well, it could involve a much larger and longer investigation. We really won't know for a couple of days."

"No problem, Luke. Just let me know if you need any help from this end."

"Will do, boss."

Each hung up knowing that they really liked the other guy.

Thirteen

The beast was, once again, already parked in the police department parking lot when Luke arrived at 7:45 a.m. Luke found Sara, once again, concentrating on her laptop. "Do you ever sleep?"

"Of course, I do, but I must admit plowing through Follett's depiction of life in tenth-century England contributed. So, what did you find out about this Steven Schmidt?"

"Well, he is a twenty-four-year-old here in Bellingham who flunked out of Western in his sopho-more year and was shortly thereafter arrested with enough Oxycontin to earn a 'possession with intent to distribute' charge. He was convicted and spent ten months in the county lockup. He appears to not have any current employment. What Simpson knows about him, along with Parker and Cruz, should be an early part of our discussion this morning. How about I take the initial lead on the whole money-laundering scheme, including the cheat sheet and the hardware wallets?"

"Fine with me. I'll jump in if I think it is appropriate. I borrowed a recorder from the sergeant out there in the bull pen. Recording on my phone really drains it of juice too fast to last what is likely to be a long session." She tucked the recorder, her notes, and laptop into her briefcase and asked Luke, "Ready to beard the lion in his den?"

Luke lifted his own briefcase. "Ready enough. Let's take a walk."

On the walk over to the county jail, Sara stopped and turned to Luke, "You know, I just have a sneaking feeling that this guy Arturo Cruz might turn out to be the key to unraveling this thing. He should already be a convicted drug dealer. He is in San Diego, as close as can be to Mexico. He routinely talks with Samuel Parker and was set free by Parker's old man. There must be a connection between him and Simpson. I'd love to know what this guy Cruz is doing."

Luke smiled. "There *is* a connection between Roger and San Diego, and it is called I-5. My grandfather used to call it the 'BC Highway': either way, it starts in BC and ends in BC—Baja California and British Columbia. Could it be as simple as getting drugs from Mexico and transporting them up I-5?"

"I don't know, but I'd sure like to know what Cruz is up to. I am going to call my office in San Diego and see if I can get some eyes on Cruz."

"Good plan," Luke replied, then stood on the sidewalk and waited for Sara to make her call. After she finished, he said, "There, at least, we are doing something. Let's go in and see what Roger Simpson has to say to us this fine morning."

***

Driving a dented 1997 Honda Accord, Jon Kienast drove past the reported address for Arturo Cruz; he did not slow down but saw nothing happening. The neighborhood consisted of small houses on small lots, all probably developed in the 1950s. Many houses had chain-link fences surrounding what had once been front lawns but were now simply bare dirt with patches of dead grass. Some residents had given up any pretense of landscaping and parked their vehicles in the yard. Most garages had been converted into additional bedrooms. The DEA agent had been on the job for more than fifteen years and had developed an uncanny ability to see things that most people would miss, but at this house, there was nothing to see. He decided to drive around the block and see if he could find some street parking where he could keep an eye on the house but finding any street parking in this neighborhood was going to be difficult. Though not ideal, he found a parking spot a block and half from the Cruz house, parked, and grabbed a paper bag as if he were simply a drunk who had pulled over and needed a few swigs to get through the day. No one noticed or cared about a drunk drinking in the privacy of his own parked car.

After fifteen minutes of apparent drinking, Jon leaned back and appeared to take a nap, though he kept one eye glued on the Cruz residence. A half an hour later, after he had nodded off once from boredom, he saw a small Econoline-sized U-Haul van pull up and back into the driveway of the Cruz residence. Jon watched as Cruz and a petite woman opened the garage and began to load the U-Haul van with moving boxes, furniture, bicycles, and trikes. Without moving his supposedly somnolent head, Jon fingered his comms button and asked for backup.

***

Luke and Sara walked into the interrogation room to find Roger Simpson sitting at the table. He was handcuffed. Luke asked the deputy to unfasten the handcuffs.

"Thanks, Agent... What was your name?"

Sara pulled out the recorder, turned it on, and announced, "This is a voluntary interview of Roger Simpson by Secret Service Agent Lucas Bitterman and DEA Agent Sara Donovan."

"Okay, so you have some questions, I guess," Roger asked.

Luke, following his agreement with Sara, replied, "Yes, we do, Roger. Do you mind if I call you Roger?"

"That's fine, if I can call you Tweedledum and Tweedledee."

"Whatever you want, Roger, but remember, if we decide that you are not be fully forthcoming, we will notify Assistant US Attorney Ennis and your non-prosecution agreement will be torn up. Can we proceed?"

"Sure, go for it."

"Okay, let's start with some simple questions," Luke said. "Do you know Arturo Cruz?"

"Nope, never heard of him."

"Do you know Steven Schmidt?"

"Nope. Not him either."

"How about Samuel Parker?"

"Him, I do know."

"How?"

"He was my attorney in Sacramento, and he is the one who got me into this mess."

"Tell us how he got you into this mess."

"Well, I was arrested on an identity theft rap, and he was appointed as a public defender to defend me. Then, after he got me ROR'd with signing an appearance bond, he told me to skip town, not show up at the trial, and come up here to await further instructions."

"Samuel Parker was your attorney and told you to skip town and set you up here in Bellingham to launder money?" Luke asked.

"You're quick, Tweedledum; that's what I said."

"How did he set you up to launder money?"

"He gave me a phone, told me to come here, and get a place to live, and that I would receive text instructions once I was settled in."

"And you received the instructions?"

"Yep, about three or four days after I got here, I got a long text with instructions from that 619 number about what to do."

"And they were?"

"To open personal checking accounts in ten or more banks, no two branches of the same parent bank. Then to wait for delivery of some cash, which I was to deposit in these banks, never more than five or six K at a time and rotating among the banks. I was supposed to chat up tellers and tell them I was a professional gambler and occasionally got lucky in some cash poker games and would be making, hopefully, several modest deposits a month. It worked like a charm. The tellers seemed enchanted to know a lucky, nice guy gambler who actually occasionally won."

Luke looked at Sara and assumed she thought the same thing he did: the gambler subterfuge was clever and an innocuous legend for having and depositing cash.

Luke continued, "So, where did you get the money?"

"A guy delivered a bag of money every Thursday night."

"What is this guy's name?'

"I have no idea, just a guy. He came to the door, handed me the bag, and left without a word."

"What did you do after you drove around and made these deposits?"

"It was simple. I bought Bitcoins at various exchanges and had them deposited into my wallet. Then, every week or so, I transferred the Bitcoins to another wallet, the number of which had been in my original instructions. But I could keep three percent of each transfer."

"Roger, the bank records in your condo showed you processed about eighty to hundred thousand dollars a month, which would leave you with only twenty-five hundred to three grand a month. That's pretty cheesy pay for committing all the crimes you were."

"Yeah, but they also transferred four thou a month in Bitcoin to my wallet as a sort of base pay, I guess. So, it wasn't that bad. Also, I figured I had enough time on my hands to start my other business, the AP Coin thing."

"We'll get to that in a while." Luke reached into his briefcase and pulled out a driver's license picture of Steven Schmidt, "Is this the guy?"

"Yeah, that him! How'd you know that?"

"Never mind. So, you sent a hundred K of Bitcoin to a wallet address every month. Whose wallet was that?"

"I have no idea. Just followed instructions."

"Okay, Roger. We found that the wallet you sent Bitcoins to had a couple of million dollars' worth of Bitcoin in it. You couldn't be the only money launderer sending money to that wallet. Do you know who or where the other launderers are?"

"Not a clue." Roger paused. "Actually, I might. A couple of months ago, I got a text from the 916 number that said, 'Effective immediately, fifty percent Bitcoin, fifty percent Ethereum,' and the addressees were 'Bham' for me and a few other cities. I don't think the guy really meant for the text to show the other recipients, but it did."

"What were the other cities, Roger?"

"I don't remember all of them, but there was LA, Sacto, Medford, Portland, Seattle, and there were a couple of others, but I don't remember."

Luke looked to Sara and said simply, "I-5." Turning back to Roger, he asked, "So what are these phone numbers you had on your cheat sheet?"

"They were numbers to be used only in an emergency. The local number was to be used only if there was a problem with the delivery of the money. The 916 number was to be used only for questions or issues about the crypto transfers."

"All right, Roger, you are doing great. You may end up walking away from most of this mess, but we have a lot more questions for you. What do you think Steven Schmidt is going to do when he goes to deliver his bag of money tomorrow and finds your building broken and nothing but cops in the area?"

"I am sure he will really freak out."

"Would you be willing to send a text to your local bag man?"

"If I have to to get out of this mess, sure."

"Here's what I want you to do: I want you to send this Steven Schmidt a text saying that your condo was destroyed in the earthquake, you are getting a new apartment, and will text him when you have a new address for the deliveries. Can you do that, Roger?"

"Sure, but I'll need my phone. He probably knows my number and has it in his caller ID system. A call from another number might make him suspicious."

"Good thinking, Roger. Agent Donovan will get your phone." Luke nodded to Sara, who returned the nod and left to retrieve the phone.

Sara returned to the interrogation room with Roger's phone and handed it to Luke. Luke told Roger that he wanted him to text the following exactly worded message: "Apartment destroyed in earthquake. Had to move. Will text you with new address soon."

Roger took the phone and texted as instructed.

Luke smiled and told Roger, "You really are doing great, Roger. Is there anything else you can tell us about the drug and money laundering that will lead us to the people who got you into this deep shit?"

"Just that I didn't have a damn thing to do with drugs. I only dealt with the money. You didn't find any drugs in my place, and I didn't ever see or deal or touch any drugs. That's on other people."

"I believe you, Roger. We are going to take a break now for about a half an hour, and when we come back, we'll want to talk to you about the American Patriot Coin project and how we can make that whole thing disappear."

"Whatever."

Luke and Sara left the interrogation room. Roger was returned to his cell with plenty of time to kill before lunch.

***

Jon Kienast started his car and pulled away from the curb, into the traffic, and out of the neighborhood. Sonja Hernandez walked down the sidewalk next to spot vacated by Kienast's Honda. She observed Arturo Cruz and his girlfriend continuing to load the U-Haul van. She stopped at the corner and sat on the bench at the bus stop for the Number 12 bus to Downtown San Diego. DEA Agent Carla Jefferson drove a truck painted with garish ads for a termite extermination company and parked in the space vacated by the Honda. She then immediately began to videotape Arturo Cruz's packing of the U-Haul van in preparation of moving somewhere. Cruz got into the van with his female companion, backed out the driveway, and drove down the street. The pest control company truck followed, stopped to pick up Agent Hernandez, and followed the U-Haul at a considerable distance. Cruz went directly to I-5 north, driving just below the speed limit.

Agent Jefferson turned to Agent Hernandez and said, "I would sure love to get a tracker on that rental van. There is no telling where or how far they are going. Hell, they could actually be moving and headed for Montana or New York."

After the moving van passed the interchange with I-8 east and stayed on I-5 north, Sonja narrowed the likely destinations. "Well, they are not going to Texas, Louisiana, or New Mexico. But you're right, a tracker would sure help."

As the van and termite extermination truck neared Disneyland, the van pulled off the interstate and parked in front of a gas station convenience store. The DEA truck pulled around the back of the store and parked near the restrooms, then Sonja said, "This may be our chance, Carla." She opened the rear doors of the service truck, grabbed a small circular transmitter, turned it on to test the battery, and smiled at the small green light that responded.

Agent Sonja Hernandez walked around to the front of the store, just as Cruz and his female companion entered the store. Whether the stop was simply a pit stop or the desire for a soft drink and a snack, Sonja knew she had only a minute or two to place the tracker. She turned toward the gas pumps and waved at a man pumping gas. "I got you your cigarettes, John." Then she walked behind the van. She leaned over and placed the magnetic tracker behind the bumper on the frame of the truck. She quickly walked back toward the front of the store, yelling toward the gas pumps, "I gotta make a stop, honey. I'll be right there." She then walked briskly to the rear of the store, seemingly headed for the restrooms.

As the van and the truck reentered I-5 north, Sonja opened her laptop and, after just a few keystrokes, told

Carla, "Okay, we got him. You can back off a bit now. I think we really need to get someone else in on this little chase. First, this truck is kind of distinctive, and second, I am going to have to stop sometime and make a pit stop for real."

In Carson, the van again left I-5 and pulled into a corner of a busy Walmart parking lot. The two agents parked seven rows of cars away and watched as Arturo got out of the van and made a call on his cell phone. Agent Hernandez also made a call. Five minutes passed with the DEA agents sitting in their truck and Arturo pacing around his van. A dark blue compact SUV pulled in and parked next to Arturo's van.

Carla grabbed her phone and said, "I think we'd better be getting video of this."

A slight thirty-something-year-old man waved to Arturo and opened the rear door of his SUV. Arturo opened the rear pull-up door of the van and climbed in.

A minute later, Arturo handed the SUV driver first one box, then another, and then three more, all of which were placed in the SUV. The rear doors on both vehicles were closed, each driver returned to his vehicle, and both drivers started their engines.

"Sonja, there's our backup," Carla said after she spotted a generic four-door Japanese car pull into the lot, with what appeared to be a young couple in the front seat.

"I'll tell them to follow and track the van. We'll take the SUV."

"Got it."

Sonja followed the SUV out of the parking lot, while Carla briefed their replacements on the van and the tracker transmission frequency. "Was that just a large shipment of drugs being transferred right out in the sunlight of the day and in the middle of a busy parking lot?"

"I do believe that that is exactly what that was,' Carla replied. "I wonder who this character is." She pointed to the SUV five cars ahead of them on the surface street. "Let's see what the plate can tell us." She phoned it in, then reported to Sonja, "The car is registered to a Carmen Ellis, five foot seven, a buck thirty, no priors, and an address in Commerce. I'll bet that's where he is headed. I know we weren't supposed to get involved, just to keep eyes on Cruz, but now we have reason to believe he had drugs in the van and this character Ellis has drugs in his car. It just doesn't seem right to be merely keeping eyes on them."

"I know, Carla, but orders are orders and if we just stay glued to these guys, it could lead to a lot more that we can roll up in one big swoop. If we jump the gun, many others might go unidentified and just melt into the pavement."

"I know you're right. But it just doesn't feel right."

Fourteen

Over lunch at a Denny's, Luke suggested to Sara that there were still several questions about the money laundering that he wanted to pursue with Roger. "It is obvious that Roger is not the only money launderer in this operation. He only handled about hundred grand a month, but the master wallet to which he forwarded the money had around two million in it. Let's hope he has remembered more of the other nodes in this system than he told us this morning. Also, we need to find out more about the lawyer in Sacramento who set all this up and what connection he and his father have with Arturo Cruz."

"Good," Sara replied. "After lunch, why don't I stop by and visit with Lieutenant Zale and tell him about Roger's text to Schmidt. Hopefully, he can keep an eye on Schmidt. I'll also roam around online and try to get more on Parker and Cruz and then join you with Roger later this afternoon."

"If you are going to further pursue the wallets, why don't you deploy Cue Lou?"

"You're right! I should have thought of that."

QLUE, the Qualitative Law Enforcement Unified Edge, allowed law enforcement, banks, and financial regulators to sort through the millions of Bitcoin and Ethereum transactions and produce a visual map of transactions involving specific wallets. It could not reveal names of the owners of the wallets, but it did present a specific trail of transactions, amounts, and wallets involved.

"We've got a plan." Luke smiled. "Maybe you should touch base with Mel and give her an update on what Roger has been telling us and what we have in place to get to the bottom of this."

"Will do."

Each agent picked up their separate checks and were back in the Bellingham Police Headquarters in ten minutes. On Luke's walk back to the county jail, he was struck with what a fine day it was in Bellingham and at the smiling faces he encountered on the walk. One giggling little girl in a stroller reminded him of Ashley, so he sat down on an available bench and phoned Annie. "Hi, love, I had a few minutes and I thought I'd phone and just check in. How are you and little miss?"

"We're both doing great, but I am beginning to worry about her being able to recognize her daddy."

Ignoring Annie's not-so-subtle request to get his butt home, Luke implored, "I certainly hope in my absence you are teaching Ashley more than that alien language you seem to enjoy so much."

"If you had been here the last few days, maybe you'd start becoming proficient in the alien language too. Any idea when you're going to be able to come home?"

"Honestly, at this point, I don't know. I'm involved with questioning a bad guy we caught, and it is going well, but I think it might still take another day or two, so maybe sometime this weekend. I think I better be able to come home soon because I don't want to wear out my welcome with Alan and Maria, though they have been most gracious. Anyway, I'll let you know as soon as I can about a return date and time. I gotta go. Just wanted to check in. You give Ashley a hug for me... and give yourself one for me too. Love ya."

"You, too, Lucas Wallace Bitterman."

Luke smiled and finished his stroll over to the jail.

***

"Hi, there, Roger. How was your lunch?"

"They'd do better by us if they drove through McDonald's and picked up fifty or sixty happy meals."

"Well, we had a great lunch, thanks for asking. Let's get back to this money-laundering scheme, could we?" Luke turned on the recorder before he continued, "Roger, you laundered about a hundred grand a month, purchased Bitcoins, and then sent it to another wallet."

Roger nodded.

"But that other wallet has about two million dollars in it. This morning you mentioned you got that message with five other recipients in five other cities: LA, Sacramento, Medford, Portland, and Seattle. Have you remembered any more cities mentioned in that message? Unless these other five sites processed more cash than you did—and that would be hard to do—there had to be more."

"Nope, sorry."

Luke pressed on, "Okay. Now about this lawyer of yours, Samuel Parker. What kind of guy is he?"

"Well, it's obvious; he is crooked. He told me to skip town and set up shop up here in Bellingham."

"Why do you think he selected you to run this operation. Hell, you had been arrested and were going to jail for being crooked yourself. Would you trust a known felon to handle a hundred grand of your money?"

"No, probably not. I think he chose me because of my computer skills. I was a computer science major in college until I dropped out, and he knew I had a sophisticated identify theft operation I conducted from my own home computer. So, maybe Parker simply needed someone with computer skills."

"Anything else you can tell me about him?"

"Not really. One weird thing, though: when we talked about my case, he quoted his dad a lot, you know, saying things like, 'As my dad used to say' or 'No good deed goes unpunished' or 'In for a penny, in for a pound'—whatever that means. That's really it, though."

"All right, Roger, let's talk about the American Patriot Coin scheme. You set up a fancy website, including a way for potential customers to purchase the offered tokens using credit cards, PayPal, and Bitcoin. I assume the Bitcoin transactions simply ended up in your wallet, while you used the PayPal payments to purchase the gold bullion coins. What about the credit card purchases?"

"Those payments went directly to my checking account, my actual personal checking account at Shuksan Savings and Loan."

"It appears that the website was established about three months ago, which is when you started chumming the waters with all those phony emails and chat room posts, starting buzz about American Patriot Coin, Inc. Is that correct?"

"Yeah, and it was working really well. People are so greedy; they jump at any chance to make a quick buck. They also don't do much checking out of things they have already convinced themselves would be a great investment. I guess they don't want to run the risk of finding out it is a scam. But people are also impatient; they want to get in and out with a big profit quickly. That's why I planned on running the website and selling tokens for only another two or three weeks. I figured investors would begin to get suspicious pretty quickly when all they got for their money was a certificate of authenticity for x tokens in AP Coins."

"So, you were only going to run the scam for another three weeks or so? Then what were you going to do?"

"I hadn't figured that out yet. I could easily just take down the website. The texts and emails were anonymized and untraceable, and the proceeds were untraceable, so I guess I could have just shut it down and stayed put until I came up with another idea. But part of me was growing tired of the money-laundering scheme, and as you said, it wasn't nearly as lucrative as the coin gig. But on that one, I would have to disappear. I don't think the folks behind all that would take kindly to a person simply giving his two-week notice and requesting a retirement party."

"No, I imagine they wouldn't. As Ms. Ennis told you, as part of your cooperation agreement, you are going to have to unravel the whole scheme. You do have a list of investors' amounts and addresses, right?"

"Yeah, I have all that: the wallet identification for Bitcoin purchases and the email addresses for all the ways of purchasing the tokens. I used the addresses to email their certificates."

"So, you can return the Bitcoins and notify the PayPal and credit card investors that the whole thing had fallen apart, and they would receive a refund for the whole amount sent to whichever mechanism they used to make the original purchase?"

"Yeah, sure. For all of it, I could simply reverse the transactions, no matter what platform was used. But if I do all that, does that mean that the agreement with the feds would hold off the SEC and the IRS, who the lady attorney mentioned?"

"That, Roger, I am not certain. But I can tell you one thing for certain: if you don't help unravel this, Ms. Ennis will have you in court on several felonies that will make the IRS and SEC interest look puny."

Luke's phone chimed the arrival of a text from Agent Sara Donovan: *"Things going active. Come to the lieutenant's office."*

"Roger, I have to leave for a while. I'll be getting back with you later today or first thing tomorrow." Luke hurried from the room.

Fifteen

When Luke entered the lieutenant's office, he saw that Tom, Mel, and Sara were already deep in conversation. "So. What's up?"

Sara was obviously excited to report to him. "My hunch about Arturo Cruz, Roger's report of some of the other West Coast cities involved in this drug distribution system, and your insight about I-5 being the conduit are all being confirmed as we speak. DEA agents spotted Cruz and a female companion loading a small U-Haul rental van with boxes and household furniture. They followed the vehicle, eventually involving several other DEA officers and vehicles, and watched as he stopped in a Walmart parking lot in the LA area and unloaded several boxes into another car and proceeded north on I-5. Agents are keeping track of the delivered shipment in LA. Cruz next stopped at a Costco parking lot in Burbank, made a phone call, and, a little while later, made delivery of several more boxes and then headed over the grapevine. Again, we are keeping eyes on the delivered product. He is now headed toward Sacramento and—we have to assume— eventually right here to Bellingham."

Mel frowned in consternation. "We, obviously, have a decision to make. Do we nab these guys after each shipment is dropped off or do we keep track as best we can and roll them all up in one large simultaneous sweep?"

Luke had never had the experience of watching a crime unfold as he was investigating it. His prior cases had, as he told his family, been rather simple—investigate, arrest, investigate some more, testify, and move on to the next case—mostly chasing numbers and paperwork. However, he felt strongly that the chance to collect information about the whole operation was more valuable than nabbing the bad guys serially and running the risk of not ferreting out the whole thing. "I believe the risk of holding off is worth the chance of getting everyone involved when we have all the facts. Right now, we have mounting evidence of the drug routes and the local dealers, but nothing solid on either the actual bosses of this syndicate or on their suppliers and the whole front end of the operation. We suspect a crooked lawyer and a corrupt judge, son and father, but at this point that is only surmise. Roger told us he thinks he was recruited by the lawyer because of his computer skills. I bet the father dismissed the case against Cruz because he was an experienced drug traf-ficker and the judge needed his skills, which leads to two conclusions: one, if the father and son are running this thing, they are amateurs and simply used their positions to get the skills and courage to do the actual work of running and collecting the benefits from a drug operation; and, two, there could be players, other recruits, involved here that we simply have no idea about."

Tom asked a logical but unasked question, "How long is that tracker likely to function?"

Sara had already checked. "It is likely to have a useful life of around forty-eight hours. Then we are back to visual surveillance only. If Cruz only takes a few minutes at each stop and there are, let's assume, six to ten more stops between where he is now and here, the battery life shouldn't be a problem. Unless he stops someplace for the night along the way. Two nights of stops, and we're in trouble."

"All right, folks," Mel concluded. "For now we keep track of the progress of the shipments coming north, and you two," she looked at Luke and Sara, "continue to get whatever information Mr. Simpson can provide. I know it is a lot to ask, folks, but I think we need to stay on top of this around the clock until it is time to pull the trigger and wrap it up. I can be reached any time day or night on my cell. Could you two continue to question Mr. Simpson and then share shifts with the lieutenant here, monitoring the progress of Mr. Cruz?"

"No, problem," replied all three simultaneously.

After the assistant US attorney left the lieutenant's office, the three officers quickly decided how they would stay on top of things. As the officers tracking the shipment were DEA, Sara volunteered to be information central, staying in touch with them and Mel. Luke would return to continue questioning Roger, and the lieutenant would return to his regular duties while staying in touch with Luke and Sara.

***

The junior senator from New Mexico, Joseph Macias, walked the almost deserted hallways of the Hart Senate Office Building from his office to that of his longest and best friend in the Senate, the senior senator from Massachusetts, Drew Fairchild. The Senate was not in session and wouldn't be for a week, but Senator Macias had phoned and confirmed his suspicion that Senator Fairchild was in his office, working during the Fourth of July break. The two senators had met when Joe had been an undergraduate at Harvard and took an economics course from then-professor Fairchild. The two men became friends, and these many years later, both ended up in the Senate. Joe reflected that in many ways the two could not be more different: Joe was the fourth son of parents who worked at low-wage jobs, whereas Drew was the only child of a Back Bay couple, with former governors and a vice-president in their family tree. Joe had worked his way up the political ladder, starting as a city council member in Santa Fe to state senator to a seat in the US House of Representatives, and eight years ago, finally to the Senate, Drew had smoothly risen directly from a Harvard faculty member to the Senate. Joe was married to the same woman for thirty years and had five children, whereas Drew had divorced years ago, had no children, and was now a devoted bachelor. But the two men were also both a rarity in the Senate and were moderates in their respective parties and considered more practical than partisan. They both were among the small handful of senators who didn't look in the mirror in the morning and see a president, and they eschewed the Sunday morning talk shows and newspaper headlines. They were also both so popular in their home states that they were assured of re-election as long as they wanted to continue to serve.

Joe knocked on the open door to Drew's office and was waved in. Their evening visits for drinks and conversation had become one of the rewards each cherished after a long day.

"So, Joe, how was your visit to the homestead? Family all good?" Drew walked over to the hidden bar and pulled out two glasses, an ice bucket, and a bottle of Knob Creek.

"Elana and kids are all fine. The big news for our family is that Richard was just accepted into the PhD program at MIT."

"That's wonderful! He is a smart young man and will do great, I'm sure. Hell, maybe he can move into your old apartment." Drew handed a drink to Joe, and they sat in facing club chairs in front of a faux fireplace.

"I am sure that dump was torn down years ago." With a grin that suggested he was kidding, Joe added, "I was thinking he could move into your house in Cambridge." Drew had three homes: his D.C. house in Georgetown, his Massachusetts home in Cambridge, and a sprawling vacation mansion on Maui.

"Actually, that might not be a bad idea at all. I am almost never there, and it just sits empty most of the time. Maybe Richard could move in and function as sort of a caretaker in exchange for free run of the place. Seriously, ask Richard if he would be interested."

"Drew, you know I was only kidding. But if you really think such an arrangement might work, I appreciate it and I will talk with Richard about it."

"So, Joe, did your visit home give you any insights about what's on the minds of those outside the beltway?"

"Predictably, most conversations start with questions about the receding pandemic and the speed of the economic recovery, but I continue to hear confusion or pushback on that virtual currency question on the front page of the tax form this year."

"Same here. In fact, I have had so many emails, letters, and phone calls about that that I have memorized it: 'At any time this year, did you receive, sell, send, or otherwise acquire any financial interest in virtual currency?'"

"Is there any evidence that the IRS is going to actually get the kinds of data they need to get a handle on this whole virtual currency thing?"

"It is too early to tell, but I certainly understand the need. The inescapable fact is that there are about two trillion dollars in US currency in circulation, and just a few months ago, the amount of wealth tied up in virtual currencies topped one trillion dollars. Most of the economic activity using real money is appropriately taxed because of our elaborate system of reporting, accounting, and surveillance, but much, if not most, of the taxable transactions in the cryptocurrency world evade taxation. This IRS effort is a reasonable and necessary step to remedy that, though there are many crypto zealots who don't like it one bit."

"Have you seen the bill that Senator Peterson is circulating?"

"I have, and I think the three major provisions are spot on and long overdue."

"Okay, you're the economist—I had a mostly super-ficial education in economics in college—so what do you think the Peterson bill would do?"

"Joe, I can't let you pin that crummy education on me—they hadn't even invented the first cryptocurrency when you were in my class. Hell, we were still using silver certificates when you were my student. But, as I see it, the Peterson bill has two important technical improvements and one major advancement of US interests. Currently, alternative currency exchanges are required to prepare a 1099 K for the customer and the IRS when more than twenty thousand dollars or two hundred transactions involving a cryptocurrency are involved. When the IRS does its document matching and finds that the exchange reported a large transaction for a particular individual and that individual does not report it, it will trigger an audit. However, for some investors, the law requires the exchanges to report with a 1099 MISC such activity when only six hundred dollars is involved. There is considerable confusion out there, and the Peterson bill would set the limit at five hundred dollars for all individuals and exchanges."

"Sounds reasonable. I know that my stockbroker reports to me and the IRS whenever I sell a stock, and it is up to me to report it and calculate whether or not there was a taxable capital gain."

"Exactly. The other technical improvement is to declare that all virtual currencies are 'securities,' which would bring all the laws, regulations, and taxes associated with the stock market to bear on cryptocurrency transactions."

"Again, sounds reasonable to me—make the crypto world conform to the securities environment. So, what is the big change?"

"Currently, taxpayers are required to report any foreign bank or financial accounts, and there are fines from ten to hundred thousand for failing to do so. The problem is that if someone sends, say, ten thousand dollars to a foreign virtual currency exchange, that exchange, unlike US exchanges, doesn't have to report it and there is no way for the IRS to determine whether or not a citizen has such an account. The Peterson bill would require that US banks report to the IRS any transaction directed to an overseas entity. This would help close a current huge loophole in the cryptocurrency world and may even help in ferreting out funding for terrorists and drug, sex, and arms trafficking."

"I have asked my chief of staff to provide an analysis of this bill, but your explanation makes it sound like a set of good ideas. Are you going to co-sponsor it?"

"I haven't decided. As you noted, there are a lot of people in this country who would view this kind of regulation as big brother stepping all over their rights to do whatever they want, but I suspect there are even more who would welcome a leveling of the playing field between traditional investors and investors in these cryptocurrencies. The thing that really perplexes me is that the US already has a digital currency."

"Okay, I'll admit I slept through a few classes in your macroeconomics class, but how it is that we already have a virtual currency?"

"Joe, I just told you that there are about two trillion dollars in actual currency, but we have another eighteen trillion dollars that we can spend—in checking and savings accounts and short-term CDs. That spendable money only exists as electronic entries in a bank and are not physical dollars. So, ninety percent of the money people can spend is, simply, already digital. I am at a loss why we need another digital currency, much less twelve hundred of them."

"I read yesterday that the Fed is actively considering joining the fray by issuing its own digital dollar."

"It is, but the rollout of that sort of thing would be really complicated and would have to be bomb-proof right from the start. However, I can see why they are considering it. The fact is that our traditional mechanisms for financial transactions—using personal checks, cashier's checks, credit or debit cards—all are slow, incur transaction costs, and are mediated by banks. Digital transactions are, or can be, secure, are instantaneous, and incur little or no cost... and most importantly to many crypto fanatics, are almost unregulated. So, the Fed is really stuck. If they ignore digital currency, they will only have control over a declining piece of the economy—government-issued paper money and bank-regulated digital resources. They probably do have to join the digital currency movement or be left irrelevantly behind. The banks are screaming like banshees and are lobbying hard to keep the Fed out of digital currencies; if a greater percentage of the economy can be conducted without their facilitation, they will literally have no future."

"So, the future of banks, cryptocurrencies, the economy, the Federal Reserve, the status of the dollar as the world's currency, and everyday citizens' daily financial transactions are all hanging in the balance, depending on what we and the Fed do in the coming months."

"I am afraid you summarized just right."

The senators switched to discussion of other issues coming before the senate, had one more drink, and went home. Joe walked to his K Street apartment and Drew called his limo to take him home to Georgetown. On their way out of the building, each chatted with Capitol police officers still shaken from the events of January 6.

Sixteen

Arturo hated driving the section of I-5 up the San Joaquin Valley. It was long, straight, boring, and had little or nothing to look at. It was tempting to speed on this stretch of road, and most people did. But Arturo knew he had to keep his speed at or only a mile or two over the posted 70 miles per hour speed limit to avoid attracting attention. Even at that speed, hour after hour, he was passed by cars, vans, and eighteen wheelers. The air conditioner refused to work.

"Damn, it is hot. It must be a hundred and five and this crappy van," Arturo slapped the dashboard, "had to be the one with the air conditioning on the fritz. Let's roll down the windows and at least get some circulation in here."

He and his girlfriend both did. It didn't help.

To relieve the boredom, Arturo began counting the number of U-Haul, Hertz, and Ryder rental trucks and trailers traveling on the highway. After only about a half hour, he had counted ninety-three such vehicles apparently moving folks from one place to another. He stopped counting but congratulated himself on how clever it was to decide to use a rental moving van to transport his deliveries. As he learned years ago on the beaches of southern California, no one notices a particular seagull in a flock of seagulls until one of them chooses to shit on your head.

Arturo kept to his driving and shifted his thinking to a problem that had been bugging him since he and Manny had picked up their last shipment. He seethed that it was *he* who ran the risk of collecting the shipment at sea. And it was *he* who loaded the van and drove to all these cities to deliver the product. It was *he* who dealt with the dealers in each city. But it was *not he* who collected the profits for all his work. Sure, sure, he got paid well, but even that was a small fraction of the money involved, as he had calculated many times. The problem was that he did not know who, in fact, was the person or persons who ended up with the money. He assumed that the judge was one of the recipients, but the judge did not strike Arturo as some kind of well-educated and wimpy drug czar. Someone else was. But Arturo knew only the product distribution part of the operation, not the people or logistics of handling all the cash.

As Arturo stayed in the slow lane up the San Joaquin Valley, he grew angrier and more resolved that he could and should do something to get a bigger piece of the pie. As the U-Haul van neared the point where the I-205 turned west to San Francisco and I-5 continued onto Stockton, Arturo tumbled to the conclusion that the one who ran the show and reaped all the profits had to be the person at the other end of the line when he texted about upcoming shipments from Mexico and the payments for the product and the skipper of the *Sunny Daze*. They never actually talked—it was all by text—but, of course, that person ran the show and probably banked all the proceeds.

Arturo stopped at a Burger King and his girlfriend went in to get them some dinner. Arturo pulled out his phone, looked up the 916 number, and wrote it on a piece of scratch paper he found in the center console. Then he googled, *"How can I find out the owner and location of a cell phone?"* and quickly read a couple of recommended articles. He then downloaded the apparently preferred app and entered the 916 number. It told him that the owner of the phone was Samuel Parker—same last name as the judge. When Arturo asked for the address of Samuel Parker, he was instructed he had to pay to get that information. He pulled out his wallet and entered a credit card number, expiration date, and security code and was immediately rewarded with an address in Granite Bay, which was also where the phone currently was. He wrote down the address on the same scrap of paper he'd used for the phone number.

He was thinking hard when his girlfriend returned with the food and said, "Hey, there, Art, what has you so deep in thought? This trip is going okay so far; no reason to worry."

"Oh. It's nothing. I was just thinking about making an unscheduled stop near Sacramento."

"Oh, yeah? You tired and want to spend the night?"

"Nope, just thinking about visiting an old friend of mine who lives in a suburb of Sacramento. He's kind of a screwball, but I like the guy. He really doesn't get along well with women, though. Maybe I could drop you off at a mall or something and come back and get you after a couple of hours. Keep your phone on, and I'll call you when I get back." Arturo pulled out his wallet and handed his companion three hundred-dollar bills, thinking that subsidized shopping should keep her happy for a while.

"Whatever you say, Art. I'm just along for the ride as the decoy wife of an innocent couple moving north anyway."

They ate their burgers and fries as they drove into Sacramento. Arturo tried to form plan. He knew the name and address of the guy who he concluded ran this whole thing and who reaped all the money. He could not just show up and reason with him for a pay raise, and a pay raise was not going to balance the risk he was running in this operation anyway. But he was going to confront this guy, and he was going correct the inequity he increasingly resented.

Just past Downtown Sacramento, Arturo took the exit for I-80 east.

***

Luke sat down opposite Roger in the interrogation room. "Sorry to have been so long, Roger, but something came up that I needed to attend to. I only have a few more questions today."

"Whatever. It's not like I have a hot date this evening that I have to get ready for. What do you want to know?"

"When you were arrested, we discovered your gold in the car... the seventy-two gold bullion coins."

"I thought we already talked about the gold. I bought it with some of the proceeds from the AP Coin thing."

"I know. But here's the deal: your financial records suggest you sent enough money to buy more than eighty coins. Did you cash in some of the coins after you bought them, lose them, or send them to someone else?"

"You're right, again. I did buy eighty-two coins, but one of the online exchanges I used to buy gold ripped me off and never delivered ten coins that I had paid for."

"How did they do that?"

"Simple, I placed my order and paid for it online, and unlike the other obviously more honest exchanges I had dealt with, they simply never shipped me the coins. I went back to the exchange's website, and it was shut down with no forwarding address. In short, some sonofabitch simply was running a short-term online scam and I was the victim. You guys really should go after those bums."

Luke smiled. "My grandfather always had an expression handy that captured almost any situation and your story reminds of one such saying, 'You really can't preach temperance from a barstool.'"

"What?"

Seventeen

"Sara, this is Rick Pearson. We've been following the van in question, but he has changed course. He got off I-5 and is now headed on I-80 east toward Reno. We... wait a minute, he just pulled off the highway and appears to be heading into a shopping mall parking lot. Stay on the line."

Sara whistled to Luke, who was sitting on the worn-out old leather sofa in the police department break room, working on his laptop. "Luke, Cruz is now heading on Highway 80 east toward Reno."

Luke jumped up and sat down at the table where Sara was seated as she turned her on her speaker. They heard Rick say, "Sara, the driver just dropped off his female companion and appears to be heading back toward the freeway." A couple of minutes passed, and DEA Agent Rick Pearson came back on the line and reported that the van was, once again, heading east on I-80.

***

Arturo followed the directions from his cell phone GPS and found the home of Samuel Parker without difficulty. He slowed as he drove past the address and, seeing what appeared to be a five- or six-thousand-square-foot house on five acres of land, concluded that this indeed was where all the money went. He pulled over to the side of the road at the end of the block and tried to concoct a plan about how to proceed. With a clarity he seldom experienced, he concluded that he was going to take over the whole operation. He did not know how the money was handled, but whatever manner it was, he would be in a position to change it. He could simply tell his contact in each city that the old way of handling money was out and that he would pick up the proceeds personally in the future. He also realized that Samuel Parker had a hell of a lot of money around and he could simply take it as well. What was he going to do? Call the police?

Arturo turned the van around and drove into the large circular driveway at the Parker residence. He reached under the seat and tucked his Glock 9 mm into back of his jeans and walked up to the massive front doors and knocked hard.

A disembodied speaker concealed somewhere around the door responded: "Who is it?"

Momentarily flustered, Arturo replied, "This is Arturo Cruz, and I am here to talk with Samuel Parker."

Samuel Parker was confused. How did Cruz know his name and address? "What do you want to talk with me about?"

"Do you really want to carry on this conversation with prying neighbors listening in? Open the goddamn door."

Samuel Parker knew it was unlikely that his distant neighbors could hear this conversation being conducted through a closed door, but seeing no option, he opened the door. Arturo Cruz walked through the door, pulled out his gun, and, for the first time in his life, aimed it at a person. Arturo closed the door and told the ashen-faced Parker, "We are going to discuss changes in how this drug operation of yours works." He pointed the gun in the direction of what appeared to be an office. "Let's go in there and have a little man-to-man chat." When they both moved into the office, Arturo said, "Is there anyone else in this house?"

"No."

"No Mrs. Parker?"

Trying to lighten the situation, Parker replied, "Actually, there are two former Mrs. Parkers, but not any current ones and no one else is here. Do you really have to keep pointing that damn gun at me?"

"I do. It tends to keep the conversation going in the right direction. Now, first, you are no longer involved, much less running, this shitty little drug syndicate of yours. I am. Second, over the last year and half, you have made millions of dollars in this little scheme, and you are now going to give it to me."

"You've got to be nuts! Why should I give you anything? And do you really think you can run this thing?"

"Both good questions, Parker. You will give me the money because if you don't, you will be as dead as that stupid deer mounted on the wall behind your desk. Should be an easy choice. Second, yes, as I am already doing all the heavy lifting on this gig, I do think I can effectively run it, and I don't need your amateur interference to make it work. So, where is the cash you've banked these last couple of years?"

Samuel quickly decided that Cruz meant what he threatened and he could soon be dead if he didn't comply. "Okay, okay, don't get all jumpy. Yes, I have a lot of cash. You can have it. Just take it... and the network... and leave." He got up to move toward the desk.

Arturo raised the gun a little higher. "No dumb moves. Where are you going?"

"To my desk. All the money is in an electronic wallet and you can have it. Just take it. I obviously can't report this to the cops, so I'll just remain silent and you can enjoy the money and the network."

"Okay, get it, and no funny business or it will be your last thought."

Parker opened the top desk drawer and grabbed a new electronic wallet he had recently purchased as a backup, shoving the wallet loaded with Bitcoins to the back of the drawer. "Here. That wallet has about two million dollars in it, and it is yours, all yours. Just take it and leave."

Arturo took the wallet and turned it over and around in his hand. He was not familiar with digital wallets. "What is this? This has money in it? Do you have to have a username and password to get into this thing like I have for my email?"

"Yes, you do. But the username and passwords are so long no one can remember them, so I have them written down on paper here in my desk. Once you have those, all the money is yours." Samuel reached back into the desk, wrapped his hand around the semi-automatic he had stored there for just such an occasion, thumbed off the safety, and pulled it out.

Arturo saw the gun before it was leveled at him and pulled his own trigger, twice. Samuel Parker staggered back against the bookcase behind the desk, slid down the wall, and died sitting on the carpet with his back against the bookcase.

Arturo was struck with how little he cared that he had just killed a man. He had not planned on it, but Parker was stupid and had killed himself with his stupidity. Arturo went behind the desk and searched the drawers until he found the paper with the wallet username and passwords, or at least, that is what he assumed the long strings of characters were. He tucked the paper and the wallet in his shirt pocket, wiped down the only things he had touched—the desk drawer and the front door handle—and walked calmly to the U-Haul van. As he drove back to pick up his girlfriend, he marveled at how easy it had been to quickly become millions of dollars richer and the boss of a drug network. This trip was really going to be worth the hassle.

As Arturo Cruz drove away from the Parker mansion, the phone in Samuel's house rang four times and went to voicemail: "Sammy, it's me. Call me as soon as you get this message. We gotta stop this. I can't take it anymore. She's gone. It's over. We gotta stop. Call me."

***

"Sara, this is weird." It was Agent Rick Pearson calling in. "After Cruz dropped off his girlfriend, he drove to a house in an obviously wealthy suburb of Sacramento, stayed there about fifteen minutes, left, and returned to the mall. He sat in the parking lot for about an hour, much of the time on his cell phone. A car showed up in the parking lot, and Cruz transferred a shipment to a van registered to a Hector Alonzo. We have people following Alonzo, but Cruz just sat there for another twenty minutes until another car showed up and Cruz again transferred several boxes. We had to scramble, but we have people on that car too. The weird thing is that the second car had Nevada plates and is registered to a guy in Reno. Finally, Cruz appeared to call his girlfriend, she joined Cruz, and they are now back on I-5 headed north. We'll stay on him, but I suspect at some point, he might just stop and get a motel or something. It is getting late and he has been driving all day; so have we. We have another team taking over in about an hour."

Sara reasoned that Cruz's reported actions meant that he had made drops for both Sacramento and Reno, his only drop not directly on I-5.

***

As Arturo drove through Redding, crossed over an arm of Lake Shasta, and into the Siskiyous, he was thinking about several ways in which he was going to change some operational procedures of his newly acquired business. He already knew he would have to change the money-handling procedure from the current one, which he did not know anything about anyway, to a new one. He initially thought that he might just have to drive up and down the coast and collect the money, but he later figured that would be a lot of work, so he would just tell the dealers in each city to mail him the money. The Post Office is always advertising, "If it fits, it ships," and Arturo always got his mail, so why not make it easy: "Mail me the money."

Two parts of the "mail-me-the-money" scheme needed to be worked out: first, he was not quite sure how much money could be jammed into a medium- or large-sized shipping box, and, second, he was not yet clear about how he would handle the millions of dollars that were going to be mailed to him. He was confident he could figure it out.

He next decided that he would need to change his order from Mexico. It seemed safer to make fewer trips on the *Sunny Daze* and fewer trips up I-5, with more product transported each trip. Besides, Arturo reasoned, you were probably just as screwed getting caught with half a ton of heroin as you were with one or two tons of the stuff.

Just before midnight, Arturo pulled into a rest stop just north of Weed, California. "Hey, babe, I have to take a leak and get some sleep, and besides, I don't want to get into Medford before about nine or so, when the parking lot at Walmart begins to fill up."

"I'm tired, too, but I don't think these damn seats tilt back far enough to get very comfortable."

Arturo pressed the button on the side of the seat and pushed back as far as it would go. "You're right: not far but far enough. Just fold up your coat and use it as a pillow and catch some *z's*."

Eighteen

Both Luke and Sara had spent the night in the police station, switching shifts of monitoring the surveillance of Cruz and catching some sleep, though there was little to follow. Cruz and his girlfriend appeared to have slept in the van at the rest stop until around 6:15, when they each made trips to the restroom and then resumed their trip north.

"Well, they are on their way again, and apparently, the tracker is still functional," Sara reported as Luke returned with cups of coffee and some donuts from the police station break room.

"If what Simpson told us is accurate, I would guess his next stop will be Medford, only about two hours or so from where they are."

Tom rushed through the door. "Things have just gotten more interesting. I was scanning the incident report feed and saw a report of a murder near Sacramento last night. Care to guess who just bought the farm?"

Luke looked at Sara and they simultaneously said, "Samuel Parker."

"Bingo! That stop Cruz made in Granite Hills was Parker's place. This morning, the cleaning woman arrived early and, after getting no response to her knock, used her key and went into the residence to find Parker in his office shot twice in the chest and quite dead."

Sara stood up and started pacing around the room. "Well, shit! Cruz murders Parker and is now driving north, and we know he likely committed the murder. We cannot just follow this jerk. We have to take him and, in the process, lose the chance to identify the dealers in the cities on the rest of his route."

"Sara, we have eyes on this guy," said Tom. "He's not going anywhere; well, he is going somewhere, but we are right on his tail."

"We were right on his tail last night when he took a detour and killed Parker," Sara replied. We can't run the risk of him killing again as we just watch him."

"Let's get in touch with Mel and see what she has to say," Luke said, then dialed and turned on the phone's speaker so Sara and Tom could participate. "Mel, this is Luke. Tom and Sara are here too. There has been a development in the Cruz surveillance that we need some decisions about. Last night when Cruz stopped in the Sacramento area, he went to Samuel Parker's house and killed him. The body was discovered early this morning by the cleaning lady when she showed up to work. He is currently still on I-5, headed north; we believe toward a stop in Medford."

Mel interrupted, "Damn it! You're right; we need to make some decisions. First, do we immediately pick Cruz up or do we continue to follow him up I-5?"

"We are divided on exactly that issue," offered Tom.

"Let me think a minute." After less than a minute, Mel returned, "Do we still have both electronic and visual surveillance on Cruz?"

"We have electronic surveillance and a close physical surveillance, but the following DEA agents are not in visual contact with the van."

"Okay, so he is not going anyplace without us all over him. If he stops, even for something as simple as gas, I want those agents to move up and keep visual surveillance. They can only back off when he is underway again and they have a good tracker signal. Do we have a battery life situation at this point?"

"We shouldn't, but it has been transmitting for about twenty-four hours, so we might later today."

"Tighten up the surveillance and let him come to us. But there are at least two other problems we must deal with. First, who's handling the Parker murder?"

Tom told her that Placer County Sheriff's department was investigating the murder.

"All right," she replied. "They will inevitably be notifying the senior Parker of the death of his son. When they do, Papa Parker might just panic and decide it would be a good time to skip town. I am going to get in touch with my counterpart in San Diego and get the FBI out to the senior Parker place with arrest and search warrants for bribery and public corruption. The second problem, it seems to me, is that we need to rethink how we take Cruz down when and if he arrives in Bellingham. He is now not just a dealer but a murderer and likely still armed. It complicates the situation. So far, Cruz has made his deliveries in crowded public parking areas, right?"

Sara nodded to Luke, who said, "That's right. A couple of Walmart parking lots and a Costco lot in Burbank."

"We can't endanger so many people by trying to take him down in such a public place. I think you three need to come up with a plan that has less potential danger to a bunch of civilians," Mel said. "How long before Cruz will actually reach Bellingham?"

Again, Luke replied for the three officers, "He is about an hour from Medford. It is another five hundred and thirty miles from Medford to Bellingham, about eight and half hours. We believe he has several more stops between Medford and Bellingham, and each stop so far has taken only about twenty minutes, so that would put him arriving in Bellingham in around eleven hours, around six-thirty or seven this evening, still light out."

"I am going to contact the US attorneys involved in his route and urge them to get warrants for each person we can identify at each delivery and suggest arrests to occur simultaneously shortly after Cruz's last stop before Bellingham. They will need statements from the surveillance teams establishing probable cause. Sara, would you handle coordination with the DEA agents and the assistant US attorneys?"

"You got it."

"I have an interview I simply cannot postpone this morning, but I will be at your location no later than one this afternoon. Is there anything else we need to decide right now?'

Luke looked at Tom and Sara, both of whom shook their heads. "That should do it for now. Thanks for your help. We'll see you this afternoon." Luke cut off the call.

"Wow! I can't believe she took the risk of letting Cruz continue with his deliveries," said Sara. "I guess you were right, Luke. I must admit, however, if this thing goes south, I think that all of us are going to find ourselves in deep kimchee."

"Well, Sara, you have two big jobs over the next few hours: continue to monitor your colleagues' surveillance of Cruz and coordinate their statements with a series of assistant US attorneys so they can get the necessary warrants. That leaves the lieutenant and I to try to figure out the safest way to bring Cruz in. That sound good to you two?"

"Yep," from Sara, and "Yeah," from Tom.

Tom turned to Luke "Let's you and I get some coffee and go to my office." Then to Sara, he asked, "Would you like us to get you anything?"

"Nope, I'm good."

Luke and Tom settled into his office with cups of coffee that were, for once, freshly brewed. "So, Lieutenant, you are much more experienced than I am in arrests of demonstrably dangerous criminals. I usually trace bank records, corporate and personal tax filings, and incorporation documents to find the bad guys. This time, we don't need to find him. He is coming to us and apparently carrying weapons and willing to use them. Is there a standard police approach that suggests itself here?"

"Not really, but we have already decided that we can't wait for him to choose a crowded parking lot. Given his pattern so far, the two most likely places he would choose would be either the mall or Fred Meyer. The Fred Meyer lot would be the first one he would come to from the south, so wherever we take him down, it would have to be south of the Lakeway exit."

"I just drove up I-5 the other day, but I don't remember what is south of that exit."

"Not much." Tom pulled out a map from his desk and laid it out on the desktop so both could see it. "North of Mount Vernon I-5 enters some low hills. There is a casino there and only a few exits before you get to Lake Samish, and then the first exits for Fairhaven and the Alaska Ferry Terminal, then the college exits and then Lakeway. So not much."

Luke stared at the map. "Does this section between the casino and Lake Samish have many accidents?"

"No, not really. It is a section where people tend to speed, so the WSP gets a good deal of business on that stretch, but not too many accidents."

"Tom, what if the state troopers got just in front of Cruz by a quarter mile or so and ran a traffic break? You know, one or two of them weaving back and forth in front of the traffic, consistently slowing and then stopping the flow, as if they were stopping the vehicles for a large wreck ahead. The traffic stops, and one of the patrolmen begins walking down the line of stopped cars and talks to each driver, as if he were explaining the traffic problem ahead and asking them to stay in their cars. Cruz would probably think it was just that, a wreck and a stopped road, and try to remain calm when the officer approached his window. If we alerted the DEA surveillance team to close right behind Cruz before the traffic stoppage, they could be there as the officer approached Cruz. If an officer and a partner drove a tow truck up the median, as if going to a wreck, a fourth and fifth officer could join the other two and, with weapons drawn and with no place for Cruz to drive, could take him down right there."

Tom thought for a moment and replied, "That is a good idea. I see only a couple of possible problems. First, for a tow truck to get close to the Cruz vehicle, it would have to be coming from the south on that divided stretch of highway, but a tow truck in that location would most likely be coming from town, not from the south. But Cruz probably wouldn't know that. Second, the timing of such an operation would have to be precise. The WSP units would have to start their traffic slow-down procedure just in front of Cruz; too early, and a zillion vehicles would be stopped, too many for the officers to reasonably and credibly walk back to talk to the drivers. Too late, and Cruz might just drive by as they start their slow-down procedure. Also, the DEA surveillance car would have to arrive at Cruz's back bumper just before the slowdown. Again, too soon, and Cruz might get suspicious about someone being right on his bumper. Too late, and they'd be too far away for the actual takedown. But I guess if everyone is in communication, we can coordinate the timing. I think that just might work. It would certainly be safer than trying to approach the Cruz vehicle in an open parking lot crammed with civilians, like the Fred Meyer lot."

"Well, we have some time to walk through this tactic before Mel gets here and set it up before Cruz gets here this evening."

"One other thing: if, when the highway gets stopped, any of the cars around Cruz has a good Samaritan with a gun who thinks the takedown is a carjacking, he might just start shooting, thinking he's averting a crime."

"If the DEA agents and the tow truck team all wore their 'police' windbreakers, it wouldn't look like a crime in progress."

"You're right. We can arrange that. I sure hope this works."

***

DEA agent Chuck Denton contacted Sara again with another report. "Sara, a further update. As I told you a couple of hours ago, Cruz stopped in Medford at a Walmart parking lot. Same routine: another van showed up and they transferred five boxes from the moving van to the local's vehicle. We have the whole thing on tape and have identified the owner of the van and got his address. Locals will stick with the delivered goods and identified driver. His next stop was Eugene, at a FoodMaxx parking lot. Same routine. We are now entering the Portland area. We will track Cruz and then hand off to the next team after this drop off, and we will stick with whatever local vehicle receives the shipment. The tracker is functioning fine. I will let you know the location of the Portland stop and when the new team has taken over."

"Thanks. Medford to Portland has been a long haul for you guys."

"Tell me about it! "

Luke walked into the interrogation room, temporary operation headquarters, with Tom and Mel just as Sara finished her phone conversation.

Mel smiled. "I gather from what I heard at the end of your conversation that Cruz is now in Portland, working his way north into a prison cell?"

"He is. So far, he has made stops in south LA, Burbank, Sacramento, and, by extension, Reno, Medford, Eugene, and soon Portland. I would guess at least two more stops before he gets here, most likely Tacoma or Olympia and Seattle. Still on track to arrive here around seven this evening. Agents have video-taped each delivery transfer and identified and stuck with recipients in each city. I have given each team the contact information you provided for the local assistant US attorneys, so they can coordinate filing affidavits for the search and arrest warrants."

"Good work, Sara. I have told my counterparts that I will notify them when Cruz approaches Bellingham, and they will execute the warrants in each city almost simultaneously, supported by local police or deputy sheriffs. Tom and Luke, have you come up with a plan for when Cruz gets here?"

Tom and Luke laid out their plan for the apprehension of Cruz for Sara and Mel.

"Great," Mel said, "That sounds like as safe and effective a plan as we have available to us, given the circumstances. Have you briefed the Washington State Patrol?"

"Not yet," Tom replied. "I wanted to wait until we could run it by you and Sara, but I will go right now and get in touch with the commander of the local WSP office. He is a good friend of mine, and I know he will be pleased to assist."

Just as Tom turned to leave, Mel stopped him, "Tom, before you go, you, Luke, and Sara should know that within the last hour, the FBI arrested Judge Harold Parker on bribery and public corruption charges. As we suspected he might, he had packed some bags, had his passport in his possession, and was clearly headed for parts unknown when the FBI showed up on his doorstep. He is currently detained in the Metropolitan Correctional Center in San Diego and will likely be additionally charged with drug trafficking and money laundering. The sad thing is that he could be charged in the murder of his own son, as the murder occurred incident to an ongoing felony in which his son and he were partners, but I doubt we will go that route. I guess all we can do now is wait."

Sara snapped her fingers. "I almost forgot with all the developments unfolding so fast. I used QLUE this afternoon and got a clear visual roadmap of the flow of money. I love that program. Did you know that there are around four hundred thousand Bitcoin transactions a day and around one point one million Ethereum transactions? QLUE sorts through all that and only reveals patterns of transactions among wallets of interest. At any rate, we knew that the first wallet listed on Simpson's cheat sheet was his. He had the digital signature and the seed words. He transferred money to the second digital wallet identified on the cheat sheet. For that wallet, he didn't have the signature or the seed words; it was just the address of where he sent the money. The third wallet identifier, for which again he had the signature and the seed words, was his own wallet for the crypto coin scam. The destination wallet was the most interesting. Over the last year and half or so, it received something like fifteen million dollars, but only had around two million in it when we first looked. Turns out that that wallet transferred millions to yet another wallet address. We know the owner of the first and third wallets is Roger Simpson. We suspect the destination wallet was controlled by the Parkers, most likely Samuel Parker. The owner of the ultimate destination wallet is entirely anonymous. It could be yet another major partner in this whole drug syndicate, or it could be an offshore bank. We just don't know." Sara smiled. "I just love using QLUE. It is like building a family tree with DNA. We know that *a* is related to *b* and both are related to *c,* but we just don't know the names of *a, b,* or *c* and have to do some more digging, but we can rule out thousands of other people as being related."

Luke and Tom looked at their watches, and Sara looked at the time on her phone. Four and half hours.

Nineteen

"Sara, this is Dave Fairbanks calling, and I have Lou Kerrins with me. After Portland, Cruz stopped for gas and some fast food and then somewhat surprised us by making a stop in Olympia. Same routine, and we have people all over the local who got the shipment. He then stopped at a large Casino right next to the freeway in Tacoma and, again, followed his pattern. We are now entering Seattle. I will let you know when he makes his next stop. Tracker still functioning, but we are a little worried about battery life on that thing, so we are keeping a bit closer tail on this guy, but not enough to spook him."

"Thanks, Dave. I have asked two more agents to join you after you leave Seattle. You can tag team with them on the way to Bellingham. You know the plan for when Cruz gets close to my location?"

"Yep, we've been briefed. I will get back to you when I have something to report."

Sara turned to update the others, only to discover that Luke had gone out for coffee and that Mel and Tom had left to talk with the WSP commander.

About two and half hours to go.

***

Just south of the exit for Sea-Tac, Dave and Lou were looking forward to handing off tailing Cruz to another team. They were behind Cruz by about a mile, and the tracker was working. Dave saw a car in his rear-view mirror that was clearly traveling around eighty-five or ninety miles per hour and weaving from lane to lane as he passed other cars. Directly in front of the DEA vehicle was a truck from a roofing company. The speeding car roared up on Dave's bumper, passed on the left, and then cut back into the slow lane, right in front of the roofing company truck, and the truck driver hit his brakes to avoid losing his front left bumper. Two bungee cords holding several ladders on the top of the roofing company truck broke and the ladders flew forward from the truck, which immediately drove over them and sent the wayward ladders right at Dave and Lou.

"Dave, look out!"

Dave didn't have time to react and drove over the ladders, blowing out both front tires and ripping out the tailpipe of his car. He struggled to maintain control of the vehicle, but he was able to bring the car to a stop on the shoulder of the highway.

"Lou, you okay?"

"Yeah, but I think I'll need to change my shorts. That was close. I thought those damn ladders were going to come through the windshield and kill us."

"Get on the horn with Sara. We've lost Cruz and have no way to catch up with him."

"Sara, this is Lou. We've lost him. We had an accident, and he is about two or three miles ahead of us on I-5 headed north into Seattle. It looks like the traffic is slowing up ahead, so he won't be able to get very far very fast, but you are going to have to get someone else to either visually pick him up or get the tracker signal."

"Lou, are you guys all right?" Sara asked.

"Yeah, but you need to get some help quick or we are going to lose him for good."

"I'm on it. Call you back." Sara ran to Tom's office and explained the situation.

He immediately got on the radio and, after only four minutes, reported, "It's okay, Sara. There was a WSP cruiser just ahead of Cruz and your guys, and he visually spotted the U-Haul stuck in traffic. He'll keep an eye on Cruz until you can get some of your people to pick up the tail."

It took longer than Sara would have wanted, but a surveillance team that was prepared to take over when Cruz left Seattle was ready and was able to pick up the Cruz tail by the time the U-Haul van reached Lake Union.

"Sara, this is Mandy Escobar, and I have Adam Mix with me. We got him. The tracker is working, and we are only about twenty or so cars behind Cruz in horrible traffic."

"Great. Stay on him. I'll get back to you in a minute."

Sara called Dave and Lou back and was relieved to learn that they were, in fact, okay. She told them that another team had successfully picked up the tail.

***

At 6:20 p.m., Arturo passed through Mount Vernon and crossed the I-5 bridge over the Skagit River. Agent Adam Mix, who had been keeping eyes on the tracking map, suddenly yelled, "Oh shit! The tracker just went dead."

Agent Mandy Escobar, who was concentrating on keeping a loose tail on the Cruz moving van, was startled. "What do you mean, 'It just went dead'?"

"Just what I said. No signal. It is not like it fell off the vehicle and is transmitting from a stationary position on the side of the road; it just went dead. I has to be the damn battery."

"Call Sara and let her know. I am going to tell the other guys to move up and keep a visual on the van."

"Sara, this is Adam. We just lost the tracker signal. Undoubtedly, the battery just crapped out. Agents Mark and Ellen are moving up to keep a visual on the van. We will hang back. When we get closer to Bellingham, we'll pull up close and they can fall a little bit back. We plan to be the ones right behind the van when the traffic is stopped, but the other team will pull up right behind us, just before the traffic stop."

"Okay, the timing in the next forty minutes or so will be critical. You let me know when the van passes the South Lake Samish exit; that will be the signal for the traffic slowdown to start. Tell Mandy to stay right behind them from that exit onward."

***

The mileage sign told Arturo that Bellingham was only fifteen miles away. He was tired after a long day of driving and deliveries, and he was anxious to get to the Fred Meyer parking lot to offload his last shipment. In addition to the planned changes to his operation he already decided, Arturo was struck by how many cities he had passed on the way up to Bellingham: Salem, Everett, Redding, Vancouver, hell, even, Mossyrock. They all had to have addicts. He corrected himself— Vancouver, Washington, certainly not Vancouver, British Columbia. That Vancouver would involve crossing the border and encountering all the risk that would involve. All he needed was local franchisees willing to push his products. He felt his planning for the new Cruz operation was going to increase sales, reduce risks, and expand his profits on the West Coast. Tonight, he would get a motel somewhere south of Bellingham on his way home and think about how to recruit some folks in all these underrepresented towns on his way home. He also was beginning to think about the millions of dollars in the electronic gizmo that he had taken from Parker.

"Art, slow down!"

Arturo saw the traffic ahead of him was slowing down, hitting their brakes, and a few hundred feet in front of the slowing traffic he saw the roof lights of two highway patrol cars weaving back and forth in front of the traffic to slow down the flow of the freeway. He had seen this before in San Diego; there must be some kind of accident ahead and the cops were slowing the traffic. The traffic continued to slow and then totally stopped.

"Don't worry, babe, there must be a wreck ahead and the cops have just stopped the traffic. I hope to shit this won't take long. I want to offload our last packages and head for home. There are too damn many trees up here for my taste."

Though it was almost seven in the evening, it was fully light in the northwest Washington summer. Arturo watched as the two state trooper cars stopped in the middle of the freeway and kept their lights flashing. One of the officers began to walk down the lanes of stopped vehicles to talk to each driver. "Look, babe, just stay cool. There is a cop walking toward us and talking to the drivers of all the stopped cars. He is probably just telling them about a wreck ahead, so stay cool. I'll talk to the guy."

In the rear-view mirror, Arturo saw more lights coming from behind him as a tow truck drove up the median toward what Arturo assumed was the wreck ahead. People in some of the cars around Arturo started to get out of their cars and try to see what the hold-up was. The two people in the car behind Arturo got out and started to walk up either side of Arturo's van to get a better view ahead, just as the state trooper got to Arturo's van and gestured for him to roll down the window. Just then the tow truck stopped, and two men climbed out.

Five officers simultaneously pulled their firearms and aimed them at Arturo: the WSP officer at the window, the tow truck team on the road in front and back of the driver's side, and two DEA agents at the front and rear of the passenger side.

"Put your hands on the wheel!"

For a second, Arturo was tempted to reach under the seat for his weapon, but he quickly realized that had been just the mistake Parker had made. His shoulders slumped, and he put his hands on the wheel. The WSP officer, joined by one of the tow truck operators, opened the door and told Arturo and his girlfriend to get out and get face down on the pavement. Arturo complied.

His girlfriend yelled, "What the hell are you doing? I ain't done nothing." She was dragged from the van and forced face-down on the pavement.

Both were cuffed and walked to the two WSP vehicles that had performed the highway stop.

Nine-year-old Margie, on vacation from California in a car next to Cruz's van, asked her father, "Why are those people in handcuffs, Dad?"

"I don't know, but somehow I am glad they are."

***

Tom, Luke, Sara, and Mel had followed the whole takedown on video feeds from body cameras. When the WSP cruisers pulled away and another late arriving WSP officer had stayed behind to direct an orderly reopening of the freeway, they each breathed a sigh of relief. Luke gave Sara an air-high five. Luke phoned Alan and asked if there was still a place at the inn and was assured there was. Before he left the police station, he phoned Annie.

"Hey, love, this is your long-lost husband. How're ya doing?"

"I was beginning to worry. I haven't heard from you for a while. Are Ashley and I becoming only dim memories?"

"Hardly. I can't wait to get home, and I think I can now definitely say that that will happen in a day or two at the most. Our case just wrapped up here, but I suspect I have a day or maybe two of paperwork before I can get on a flight home. The important part is that it is over. We got the bad guy. And I have a ton of reports to file. I am going to spend another night or maybe two with Alan and Maria. I'll let you know when I know exactly what time I will get home."

"You better get home soon, or you are going to miss Ashley's first steps."

"What? That can't be true. Last time we talked she was just making her first attempts at crawling and now you are telling me that she might be walking in the next couple of days?"

"Well, maybe not that soon, but she is a fast learner. She takes after her mother."

Luke could see the big smile at the other end of the line and, once again, knew that all was well with the world.

Twenty

Overnight teams of DEA agents, with either deputy sheriffs or police officers, raided ten locations in Los Angeles, Burbank, Sacramento, Reno, Medford, Eugene, Olympia, Tacoma, Seattle and Bellingham. Twenty-four individuals were arrested and almost nine hundred pounds of heroin and just short of a half million dollars of cash were seized. Bank records, electronic devices, drug paraphernalia (scales, plastic baggies), and thirty-six weapons were seized. In Tacoma, a fleeing person fired at officers and return fire put the suspect in a local hospital.

Early Friday morning, Luke arrived at the Bellingham Police Department, and again, the beast was already in the parking lot. Luke knew where he would find Sara but was surprised to see the workroom they had been using for almost a week now empty. Carrying his coffee, he went to the lieutenant's office, and found Tom and Sara deep in conversation. "I guess I am going to have to get up much earlier to ever have a chance to beat you two to work. What's up?"

"Good morning, sleepy head. Tom and I were just discussing what needs to be done to wrap this thing up. You and I need to get together with Roger Simpson and unravel his phony crypto scam. All of us have a lot of reports we need to write. I need to offer some advice to the nine teams about digital wallets and cheat sheets to look for. The Placer County Sheriff's Office has reported that they found the master digital wallet in Samuel Parker's desk, which they can probe with the cheat sheet discovered on Cruz. Cruz isn't talking and neither is Judge Harold Parker."

"I was thinking about the reports too. If Simpson assists us in unraveling the crypto scam, there will be no scam and, therefore, no need for a trial-ready report on that. If Mel follows through on her agreement with Simpson about making the money-laundering operation go away, there will only be need for a cursory 'memo-to-file' report on that. Our role coordinating and directing the surveillance of Cruz as he traveled up I-5 will require reports to establish the nexus between what we learned from Simpson, our initial surveillance of Cruz, and the subsequent transfers of drugs in each city."

Tom chuckled. "You know, the Cruz trial is going to have testimony from more than a dozen DEA agents, several police and sheriff's departments officers, the Secret Service, the FBI, and god knows who else."

"I agree that we need to do all the reports and everything, but there are several pieces of this puzzle that still bug me that we just don't know," Luke said, and Sara and Tom looked at him as if he were trying to rain on their parade. "Really. Think about it. First, we don't know how the judge communicated with Cruz to propose and get agreement on the scheme of trading his release on that bullshit motion to dismiss for him running a drug enterprise. That is, how did he 'recruit' Cruz? I've reviewed the trial transcript and there is nothing there. The judge would be scared to death of having an *ex parte* conversation with Cruz, as it could get him impeached. Cruz didn't just magically divine the chance to run a drug ring in celebration of being released. So how did it happen?

"Here's another one: Where and how did Cruz get his supply of heroin? Living in San Diego—National City, to be precise—it is easy and probably correct to conclude he got them from Mexico, but how? Finally, how is it that a father and son, the former a judge and the latter a lawyer, suddenly decide that it was time to start a drug syndicate? Neither one had any prior criminal history, and both had reasonable incomes. Each of them had a lot to lose."

Mel knocked and walked into Tom's office, smiled, and teased, "You guys started writing reports yet?"

"Just about to, but Luke here just raised some interesting questions and holes in the picture of this whole event. Luke, why don't you tell Mel your thinking about the several important unknowns?"

He repeated his reservations.

"Well, gang," Mel replied. "I can absolutely complete the puzzle on two of your concerns. Last night when I interviewed Cruz, I told him that he was going to be charged federally for the murder of Samuel Parker, and under 18 USC Section 36, 924(i), the penalty, upon conviction, is anything up to the death penalty. I told him that we would take the death penalty off the table in exchange for certain information. First, how was he recruited by the judge? Our case against the judge is weak without the mechanism of the bribery and corruption. Second, how and where did he get his drugs? I don't think Arturo Cruz has much interest in facing the death penalty because he immediately provided answers to both my questions.

"He told me that his brother-in-law, Manny something-or-other, visited him in detention and told him that some guy said he could get Arturo off if Arturo would agree to go to work for them."

Sara laughed out loud. "What a swell guy. At the first chance to serve himself, he throws his brother-in-law under the bus! So, any idea who this 'some guy' was that talked with Manny what's-his-name?"

"No, but Manny is being picked up as we speak, and I suspect, when given the chance, he will identify Samuel Parker as the one who approached him with the deal for Cruz. As you correctly reasoned, Luke, it could not have been the judge. Cruz's lawyer has a flawless reputation, except for writing bullshit motions, so it had to be young Parker. He probably made the offer when he was down for a visit with dear old dad."

Luke saw all the pieces finally fitting together to make a coherent picture. "So, what was the second piece of information Cruz gave up?"

"More bad news for Manny. Cruz said that he and Manny took fishing trips on a charter fishing boat called the *Sunny Daze,* and in the middle of the night and about eight or nine miles offshore, a boat delivered the drugs to them, around a half ton each trip. Again, as we speak, the owner-skipper of the *Sunny Daze* is being arrested and his boat searched, and, eventually, probably seized. Now Manny has a raft of major drug trafficking charges, in addition to bribery and interference with a judicial proceeding."

"I don't think those two brothers-in-law are going to be exchanging Christmas cards in the future" offered Tom with a satisfied grin.

Mel continued, "As to your last question, Luke, I do not have an actual answer, but I have a hunch. Samuel Parker was a mid-forties, a twice-divorced lawyer, practicing at the low rent end of the legal profession. He didn't make much and what he did make or save for retirement was probably split with his exes. He defended a lot of creeps who, even though they were caught by the time Samuel Parker knew them, had succeeded in making some big bucks engaging in illegal activity. Papa Parker was a long-serving judge who, like his son, didn't make a fortune and was approaching retirement and a good but not extravagant pension. His wife died a couple of years ago, and the judge was pretty much of a loner, with no known hobbies or commitments. Like his son, the judge saw a whole lot of crooks and how easily they had made a whole lot of money. Given all that, I suspect that father and son were both discontented with their lives, figured they deserved more rewards for their legal labors, faced a not-very-enjoyable financial future, and knew, from personal experience, that some crimes paid very handsomely, if only they could recruit people to do the work of running a drug syndicate. Both had access to a pool of people who had the requisite skill sets. So, over Christmas dinner or a Fourth of July barbecue, and probably a few drinks, Samuel proposes to Dad that they start a new business, get in for just a year or two, collect several million dollars to correct the injustices they felt life had dealt them, and bail when the coffers were full enough and before they got caught."

Luke nodded his head. "You know. I think that might just be it. Two depressed amateurs seeking to make a quick hit and get onto a better life. But Samuel Parker isn't around to confirm your guess, and I doubt the judge is going to say anything to anybody anytime soon. Fortunately, their motivations for starting and running their drug enterprise are not necessary or even relevant factors facing the judge and jury. So maybe, we will never know for sure, but, Mel, I think your take on this is probably as close to accurate as we will ever have." Luke broke into a broad grin.

"What's so funny, Luke?"

"Not funny, actually, just a memory. When I was in law school, I was assigned to write a paper on the difference between bribery and extortion. After all the subtleties are considered, I concluded that the difference was simply what was being offered in exchange for some benefit. If someone proposes to offer a benefit for some requested behavior, it is bribery, such as, 'If you give me a building permit, I will give you five hundred dollars.' If someone suggests, 'I will break your leg unless you give me a building permit,' it is extortion. We don't know how Cruz was recruited and we do not know if the judge committed bribery or extortion. It could have been either: 'If you don't run our drug network, I'll put you away for life' or 'If you run our drug network, I'll release you from your current charges'—classic splitting of legal hairs. Either way, both extortion and bribery are covered under 'public corruption.'"

It took the rest of the day that Friday for Luke, Sara, and Roger Simpson to unravel the American Patriot Coin/token digital currency scam. The gold was sold, and the proceeds were reimbursed to those who ordered tokens using PayPal and credit cards. Those who bought their token with Bitcoins were refunded with Bitcoins transferred back to the wallet from whence they came. The AP Coin website was taken down. Except for a lot of strange emails and texts floating around in the ether, AP Coins ceased to exist. There was no crime, and there were no victims. At the end of the day, Tom told Roger

Simpson that the next day, Saturday, he was going to be escorted back to Sacramento by US Marshalls where he would face the original identity theft charges and an additional charge of failure to appear. Having already skipped one trial, he was going to be held in detention without bail until his trial. The IRS also was going to be speaking with him.

Sara and Luke agreed that they could finish their report writing from their respective homes and file them electronically. Both pulled out their cell phones and got plane reservations for the next day: Luke back to San Francisco and Sara to Portland.

They left the police station, and as they approached the two vehicles parked side-by-side, Luke told Sara, "Well, DEA Special Agent Sara Donovan, it was a pleasure to work with you again, but let's not do it again anytime soon. I hate being away from home this long."

"Back at you, Secret Service Special Agent Lucas Bitterman. We are a good team, but I agree, we shouldn't make a habit of it."

Each looked awkwardly at the other and then simultaneously extended a hand.

Luke drove his cramped subcompact to Lake Whatcom for one more night with Alan and Maria. Sara drove the beast to her motel for another round of tenth-century England with Ken Follett.

Twenty-one

On the way to the Washingtons' lakefront condo, Luke stopped and bought a six-pack of Rainier, six assorted bottles of wine, a six-pack of non-alcoholic light beer, a loaf of French bread, and some sugar-free syrup. He had not spent as much time with Alan and Maria as he would have liked, but it was probably becoming a burden for them to try to make meal plans around a guy with such a screwy work schedule. Tonight, his last imposing on them, however, he could fully relax and attempt to be a good guest.

Alan answered the door with his characteristic big grin. "Hey there, Double O Seven. Were you involved in that capture of the murderer-drug trafficker?"

Luke walked past Alan to the kitchen, unpacked the wine bottles, pulled two bottles of Rainier from the six-pack and one bottle of non-alcohol beer, and put the rest in the refrigerator. "You know me well enough, Al, to know that I tell a much better story with a beer in my hands, and I've learned you are a much better listener with one in yours." Luke handed Alan a beer.

"Maria is taking a nap. Let's go out on the deck, and you can tell me all about your derring-do."

When both were seated facing the lake, with its small wind-driven whitecaps, Luke burst Alan's balloon. "I wasn't involved in the arrest of that murderer—that was the state troopers and DEA agents—but, by all accounts, the bad guy was really a bad guy and it is a good thing they caught him when they did. After the mine tunnel collapse, the last thing Bellingham needed was a gun-toting drug dealer on the loose."

"So, if you weren't involved in that, what case have you been working on and how is it going? Probably not as exciting as taking down a criminal bigwig, huh?"

"Actually, I am finished with my case as of today. Almost a week of work, and the whole case just went up in smoke: no crime to investigate and no one to arrest. So, I am going home tomorrow. I have a flight out of Sea-Tac tomorrow afternoon, around three thirty."

"Are you just putting me off? Really? You weren't involved in that big takedown? You spend untold hours and gobs of tax-payer money investigating something this last week that you now tell me was all for naught. So, you're just going home?"

"Yep, Al, that's what I'm telling you... well, kind of. Some of the work I did—sort of like analysts' work in the background—contributed to the takedown here and to breaking up a drug-trafficking operation in ten cities between here and San Diego, the arrest of a crooked judge, and the seizure of a luxury fishing boat for drug smuggling. All without having to pull my gun once."

"That's more like it! That's the Luke I know, hit a single to set the plate for me to hit the homer and drive us both in."

Maria opened the slider door and joined Luke and Alan. "I assume it was you who thoughtfully brought me a non-alcohol beer?"

Luke nodded.

"Thanks. I keep reminding Al to pick up some, but impending fatherhood seems to have affected his short-term memory."

"You didn't nap long, hon," Alan said.

"Nope, junior went on one his kick-boxing workouts and woke me up, but if I slept any longer, I wouldn't be able to go to sleep tonight, so it was a good thing he was my alarm clock. So, Luke, were you involved in that arrest out on the freeway that is all over the news?"

"I was just telling your husband here that I was very peripherally involved in getting some information about the whereabouts of that guy. So, now my work is done here, and I'll be flying home tomorrow afternoon. There are more bad guys to arrest in California than there are up here in your beautiful Northwest. Have you gotten any more word about your guys getting back out to sea?"

Maria's smile matched her husband's. "We have, in fact," Maria replied. "The company has scheduled one of our most popular Alaska cruises for the end of August. They are right now promoting the heck out of it and offering the trip for about seventy percent of the pre-pandemic price. We should know pretty soon whether the sale price and more than a year of no cruises sailing will bring in the customers or they are still too scared to gather in groups of twelve hundred and go sailing."

Alan added, "I am supposed to report to Vancouver in two weeks to shake the mothballs out the engineering systems and make sure the *Nieuw Statendam* is ready to sail if they actually get paying customers. Maria will join the ship two weeks after I do."

"I feel a little guilty about being back on the payroll, only to be planning on taking maternity leave after the baby is born. There are still so many cruise directors not yet called back. But I could not pass up the chance to be back at work, no matter how briefly it will last."

"Oh, crap!" Luke said. "Talking about how long work will last, I just realized I haven't told my boss I am flying home tomorrow. I better text him. I'll be just a minute."

As Luke finished his texting, Maria's phone rang and she answered, "Oh, hi, Mom. What's up?" Maria turned to Luke and her husband and mouthed the words, "This will take a while," then pointed to the kitchen.

"Her mother used to phone about once or twice a week until she learned that she is going to be a grand-mother. Now, she phones almost every day, and she and Maria usually gab for at least a half an hour. They have always been a close family, but this baby thing seems to have turned up the familial temperature."

"I know. Ashley had the same effect on Annie's mom and, for that matter, on Annie as well. They, too, chat quite often, which is all fine with me. Annie enjoys it and I really like her mother and father. You know, Al, you asked about my investigation up here, and as I said, I really can't comment on that, but I do have a question that a smart guy like you could help me puzzle out."

Alan cocked his head and told Luke, "Sure, buddy, what can I help you with?"

"Well, as I told you, most of the case I was working on simply went up in smoke as the result of a coop-eration agreement. We caught the guy red-handed and had ample evidence to convict him and send him away for a long time, but because he could lead us to bigger and more dangerous fish, he basically got to walk away. As I see it, law enforcement—that would be me—did its job, but the criminal justice system—that would be the assistant US attorney—traded in all our work and the prison term the guy was facing for information that led to the arrest of a whole bunch of people."

Alan interrupted Luke's characterization of his problem. "Luke, you have asked the right guy—a black guy—about the difference between law enforcement and criminal justice. I have a lifetime of experience to draw on. However, I suspect my perspective on the issue is quite different from yours."

"How so?"

"How many times have you been pulled over by police and been questioned about why you were driving in a wealthy neighborhood at night?"

"Never."

"Well, I have—four times—and each one was scary. So, on the law enforcement side of the issue, I can tell you that law enforcement is not equally enforced. You know as well as I do that drug laws seem to get black folk arrested at a much higher rate than white folk. Whites do a line of coke in the restroom of an upscale restaurant without much fear of arrest, but blacks shoot up in a back alley or flop house and have a high probability of being arrested."

"Al, I know that is all true, but what I am getting at is that even when law enforcement does its job equitably, the criminal justice system seems to only sporadically mete out justice: sometimes it lets scumbags off, and sometimes it delivers sentences much harsher than either the law or the circumstances of the arrest warrant."

"I was getting to that. Again, from my perspective, one explanation is simple. When white folks commit white collar crime and net millions in ill-gotten gains, they often get house arrest or minimal time inside a country club prison and do a couple hundred hours of community service. When a black kid robs a 7-Eleven and runs away with ninety dollars and gets caught—*whammo!*—into the jail for a long time, with no option for a country club prison, home confinement, or community service, just hard time."

"You don't need to convince me that the enforcement of laws and the service of justice are both unequally administered, but what I am talking about is the inherent tension between law enforcement and criminal justice, even if each were perfectly administered. It just seems to me that those who catch the bad guys and are, therefore, most knowledgeable about the circumstances of the crime and the criminal should have a bigger say in the ultimate determination of what would be just in a particular case. Stealing a car and going on a joy ride is different than stealing a car to take a sick child to the emergency room, but by the time they go to trial, it looks like both crimes were the same—stealing a car."

"Luke, it sounds like your law degree and your law enforcement training and experience are colliding. Maybe you should become a judge: one who knows that stealing a car is illegal but would be interested in the who's and why's in determining a punishment."

"Al, I am not consumed or depressed over this, and I certainly don't want to become a judge; I would really get fat sitting on my behind every day all day. No, my interest in this tension between the two parts of a civil society is mostly an intellectual one—an interesting dilemma. The issue you raised—equal justice under both law enforcement and the law—is, however, more than an intellectually interesting issue. It needs to be corrected or the whole interesting civil society question becomes moot."

Al's broad smile returned. "See, I solved your problem and gained a recruit to the movement for justice under the law!"

"Al, I was already a recruit and you know it. And I still can't seem to see a way that law enforcement and criminal justice can be complimentary, rather than inconsistent parts of one system. But I appreciate your help. By the way, I want a University of Tasmania T-shirt for Christmas. Have you ever been to Tasmania in your travels around the world?"

"As to the T-shirt, I think I can arrange that. They have a great one with Mumford the Lion hoisting a large mug of beer. What? An extra-large or XXL?"

Luke gave Alan the finger.

Alan smiled and added, "As to ever visiting Tasmania, no, I haven't, but Maria has, twice. Every year Holland America has one or two thirty-day cruises that circumnavigate Australia and one of the stops is Tasmania. She tells me that it really is a beautiful and interesting place, quite different from the mainland of Australia—hilly and even mountainous, heavily forested, small population, and, as far south as it is, much different agriculture than the rest of Australia."

Maria returned to the deck and told Alan, "Hon, sorry to have taken so long with Mom, but you better fire up the coals for the barbeque if we are going to eat tonight."

"Will do. Luke, we couldn't let you go home without having some of the best salmon anywhere. In season, we stop by a fish market out at the marina and pick up fish so fresh they are still looking for a stream to swim up."

Luke replied, "And I couldn't leave without having you and Maria experience my famous French toast breakfast, so while you fire up the barbecue, I am going to go in and slice a loaf of French bread so it will be ready in the morning."

Twenty-two

When Luke woke up on Saturday morning, he was surprised to note that it was 7:30. He had slept well and long and felt as if his accumulated stress and tiredness of the last week had been purged. He showered, shaved, dressed in causal khakis and a short-sleeved shirt, then packed his bag before he went to the kitchen, chasing the smell of freshly brewed coffee.

"Well, good morning, Double O Seven. All that arresting and seizing must have really pooped you out."

"All in a day's service. I know the nation is grateful."

"I was just watching the news and saw that while you guys were bringing a drug dealing murderer to justice, DEA agents arrested a few dozen drug dealers in nine or ten cities, including Bellingham, and scooping up about a ton of heroin. I imagine that Sara had something to do with that."

"It was a half a ton."

"So, you WERE involved! Come on, buddy, tell me the whole story."

"If I did, I'd have to kill you."

"Killjoy!"

"So, do you want my world-famous French toast breakfast or are you just going to prattle on? I better have a cup of coffee first, and I can't really start breakfast until Maria is up and ready for a treat."

After breakfast, Luke thanked Alan and Maria for their hospitality and wished them well in their upcoming cruise and child.

As Luke retrieved his carry-on bag and they all walked to the front door of the condo, Alan told Luke, "Hey, buddy, since you have plenty of time to make your afternoon flight out of Sea-Tac, you should see some of Bellingham on your way out of town. I would recommend that you drive up around Western—it really is a pretty campus—and then drive through Fairhaven. It is a charming section of town that was originally one of the four towns that combined to make Bellingham. It was in derelict decline for years until some years ago, people came in and redeveloped it into a vibrant collection of restaurants, art galleries, bookstores, and bead shops. From there, you can take Chuckanut Drive. It's a windy road cut into the cliffs above Puget Sound and connects with I-5 at Burlington for your trip south. Sections of Chuckanut remind me of Highway 1 around Big Sur. You'll love it."

After he left his friends, Luke followed Al's recommendation and drove around the periphery of Western and appreciated the small college feel of the campus that Alan had told him had begun operation in 1893 as the New Whatcom Normal School. He wound down the hill to State Street and headed for Fairhaven. Luke concluded that Alan was right; the whole redeveloped Fairhaven district was charming. Though he had coffee with breakfast, he decided he would park and pick up a cup of coffee for his trip south.

In the second block of walking around and playing tourist, Luke spotted a busy coffee shop and, as he entered the shop, was struck that this coffee shop seemed to cater to the last indigenous population of hippies left in the country: long-haired, sandal-wearing young people in tie-dyed T-shirts and army jackets with peace symbols painted on the back. The walls were covered with posters advocating love and peace, a Janis Joplin concert, and a "Eugene McCarthy For President" poster. Luke was sorely tempted to pull out his phone and take a few pictures, but he decided the patrons might take exception to being recorded like pandas at the zoo. The smell of freshly brewed coffee was mixed with the unmistakable smell of pot, which was being sold at the back of the shop. Luke ordered a cup of coffee, asked for directions to Chuckanut Drive, and left the cultural time capsule to continue his trip south to his plane home.

On his way to his rental car, Luke passed a bookstore too tempting to pass up. Luke wandered around the store and was attracted to a book titled, *Poetry of the Northwest*. He thumbed through the pages and was attracted to a poem called *Northwest Rivers*, by Eugene S. Fairbanks. The very first word was one his brief time in the northwest had introduced to him.

> Snohomish, Wenatchee, Stehekin,
> Quinault, Okanogan, Puyallup,
> Nespelum, Skokomish, Nisqually,
> Snoqualmie, Palouse, Dosewallips—
>
> gather moisture in the mountains,
> mingle rain with summer snowmelt.
> Fed by streams that trickle downward,
> cold and clear, the waters chatter.
>
> Santiam, Wallowa, Cle Elum,
> Pysht, Skagit, Ozette, Hamma Hamma,
> Skykomish, Newaukum, Humptulips,
> Snake, Yakima, Kootenai, Satus—
>
> cascade down through twisting canyons,
> scour massive granite boulders,
> plunge themselves from rocky ledges,
> leap and roar like raging beasts.
>
> Spokane, Umatilla, Willamette,
> Hoh, Clakamas, Coos, Stillaguamish,
> Naselle, Walla Walla, Washougai,
> Chehalis, Wynoochee, Tucannon—
>
> tumble through the wooded foothills,
> ply vast stands of fir and hemlock—
> habitat for elk and eagles,
> spawning beds each fall for salmon.

Sauk, Skookumchuck, Klaskanine, Soleduck,
Queets, Klickitat, Quillayute, Umpqua,
Chelan, Bogachiel, Tahuya,
Twisp, Entiat, Elwha, Kalama—

wend their way past peaks and ridges,
drain broad fertile inland valleys,
join themselves one with another,
carry silt to distant shores,

Copalis, Teanawan, Klamath,
Similkameen, Toppenish, Nooksack,
Chinook, Calapooia, Lochsa,
Duwamish, Molalla, Tahoma—

nourish wetlands at their margins,
spread high water over lowlands,
seek out bays and estuaries,
cycle rainfall to the ocean.

Luke was charmed by the poem and bought the book. Once in his car, he considered phoning Annie to tell her about his encounter with the Summer of Love re-enactors, but he decided he would wait to tell the story until he got home—Ashley would probably like to hear it too. Luke started the car and headed toward the beginning of Chuckanut Drive—another word unique to the northwest idiom?

Luke was so impressed by both the twisting scenic drive and the views that he stopped at three of the pull-outs just to spend some time looking at the San Juan Islands and the numerous commercial and recreational boats cruising in seemingly every direction. On a hair-pin curve, deep in a heavily treed canyon, he passed the Oyster Bar Restaurant and, moments later, saw mountains of oyster shells on the beach below, graphically certifying the freshness of the restaurant's offerings. As Alan had told him, Chuckanut Drive eventually ended near Burlington and Luke joined I-5 going south toward Seattle.

An hour and half later, he appreciated that, being midday on a Saturday, the traffic in Seattle was not bad at all. He arrived at Sea-Tac, returned his rental car, and had a couple of hours to kill before his flight to San Francisco. After clearing TSA, Luke spied a vacant seat in one of the concourse bars and grabbed it, ordered a beer, and his mind returned to one of the pieces of the puzzle that just didn't feel right.

Mel had suggested that the senior and junior Parkers were just two disgruntled single men, resenting their financial stations in life, and looking to secure the future they felt they deserved by making a relatively quick and lucrative foray into the drug trade. Though that explanation might be accurate, it just did not seem reasonable. Neither Parker had any criminal record, not even a speeding ticket, Luke guessed. Both men knew and practiced the law and had to know that such an undertaking was a high-risk and low-probability-of-success enterprise. Finally, the money, so far as they had been able to determine as the investigation unfolded, just did not add up. Samuel Parker's digital wallet had around two million dollars in it. If he were the CFO of the organization and collected transferred cryptocurrency from each of ten sites and each site was kicking out around a $100k a month, that would be about a million a month or $12 million a year. If the trafficking started when Arturo Cruz was kicked free by the senior Parker, that meant that the operation had been up and running for about two years, or around $24 million worth. With only around two million in the digital wallet found in Parker's house, that left several million dollars unaccounted for. Admittedly, they had to pay to get their supply of drugs from Mexico, and the young Parker had purchased a McMansion within the last year, but that still left a lot of money unexplained. The QLUE map documented that the junior Parker routinely transferred a lot of money from his wallet to some other wallet. Whose? Why? Another principal in the syndicate? Some entirely different enterprise they were not even aware existed? Luke knew he needed more information to follow the money to where it always led—the top of the criminal enterprise.

"Mel, this is Luke."

"Hi there, Luke, I thought you were back in San Francisco already."

"I am at Sea-Tac, waiting for my plane right now. I hate to bother you, but I am still bugged at some financial inconsistencies in our case and was wondering if you could get a subpoena for both Parkers tax returns and bank records for the last five years."

"I already have on all accounts and should have them sometime Monday morning. We have not decided whether we are going to charge the judge with money laundering, but if we do, we need those records for both the Parkers. If you like, I could shoot them to you in San Francisco."

"I'd appreciate it. By the way, do you have the name and phone number of the FBI agent who is overseeing the investigation on Parker senior?"

"Sure, hold on a minute. Yep, here it is—Ryan Bell, 619-111-8878. What do you want from him, if you don't mind my asking?"

"In addition to digging more deeply into the Parkers' finances, I'd like to learn more about the judge as a person. I just can't see him and his son spontaneously hatching the scheme to become drug czars."

"It is odd, but they did run a drug ring until Cruz killed young Parker and took over, and they did launder the proceeds from the sale of drugs. If you can ferret out why they did so, other than the obvious of wanting to make some money, I would be delighted to be enlightened. Good luck, Luke. By the way, it was great working with you and Sara; as a team, you guys are good. I'll be letting your respective superiors know that. Thanks."

"Thanks, Mel. We appreciated working with you and Tom, too. Things worked out pretty well for a situation that went so quickly kinetic, like building an airplane while flying."

"You take care."

"You, too."

No sooner had Luke put his phone in his pocket than he heard the chime of an incoming message. Annie had texted him: "No need for you to take a Lyft home. Your mom and Harrison insisted on taking us all to dinner at Camille's as a welcome home dinner celebration. Little miss and I will be hovering in the cell phone lot. Just give me a call and I'll pick you up. Love you a ton... and Ashley wants to show her daddy how she can crawl."

After responding to Annie's text, Luke phoned the number of the FBI agent that Mel had given him.

"Bell, here."

"Mr. Bell, this is Lucas Bitterman. I am a Secret Service agent and was involved in the initial investigation that led to the drug ring and the arrest of Judge Parker. I have a couple of questions about Judge Parker if you have a minute."

"Sure, fire away."

"Really, I am trying to get a handle on how the judge got involved in this whole thing to begin with. Have you interviewed any family or close friends who could shed light on what motivated the judge?"

"From what we've been able to unearth, the judge had no close friends; he was a totally devoted family man—husband and father—and dedicated to his work on the bench. The only person who seems to have any insight into Judge Parker the person was his bailiff, who had been assigned to the judge's court for about the last six years. Other than him, no family beyond his kid and wife and no close friends."

"Do you have a name and contact number for the bailiff you mentioned?"

"Sure, just a minute." Luke waited until Mr. Bell said, "Here it is. The bailiff's name is Clyde Simmons, and his number is 619-511-2938. He is really busted up over the murder of the judge's son and the arrest of the judge. He apparently really admired him."

"Thanks. I'll give him a call."

"Anything else I can do for you, Agent Bitterman?"

"Yeah, actually there is. I understand that there were no digital currency wallets found in the judge's residence or on his person when he was arrested. Is that right?"

"Yes. The judge appeared to be strictly old school. He had an old computer but appeared to use it only for email. He didn't do his banking or bill paying online; he made trips to the bank and mailed checks for his bills. In fact, other than the obvious crime of corruption in falsely releasing Cruz in order to recruit him to run the drug network, we have found no evidence of drug trafficking or money laundering."

"Thanks, I think that answers all my questions. I think I'll phone Mr. Simmons and see if I can clear up some confusion on our end of things. Thanks for your help."

"Sure thing."

Luke dialed the number for the bailiff and was pleased to receive a "Hello."

"Mr. Simmons, my name is Lucas Bitterman. I am an agent with the Secret Service and have a few questions I hope you can help me with. Do you have time now?"

"Sure. Secret Service, you say? I have already talked with the FBI. Maybe you should be talking with them. I told them everything I know."

"Thank you, Mr. Simmons. I just have a couple of questions that concern how the judge got himself into this mess he is in, and I understand that you might be the person closest to him and might be able to answer our questions."

"Mr.—What was it?"

"Bitterman."

"Mr. Bitterman, I have no idea what led to the judge's arrest or the murder of his son, for that matter. They are... or were... nice guys. The whole family was. I served in his court for about six years, and he was a real good judge. Competent. Fair. Hard working."

"Did that include the Cruz trial?"

"Now that was the only sour note. I ain't no lawyer, but I bet I have heard more cases than most lawyers. That case appeared to have been a slam dunk, and then, out of the blue, the judge goes and dismisses the whole thing and lets Mr. Cruz walk out of the court-room. I never saw anything like it before—or since. I don't know what the judge was thinking, but I suspect he had his reasons. I just couldn't figure out what they were."

"What kind of person is the judge? How was he to work for?"

"He was all business. Always nice enough to people like me and the court reporters. Totally dedicated to his family. His wife used to come and sit in court and watch the judge work. So did his son, occasionally. The judge's office must have had fifty or sixty pictures of the family—his wife, his son, all three of them together."

"How did he get along with the lawyers who appeared before him?"

"Almost all the lawyers—both prosecutors and defense attorneys—liked drawing the judge for their cases. Like I said, he was fair, competent, and reasonable. What is going to happen to the judge?"

"I do not know, Mr. Simmons. I appreciate your insights into the judge. Is there anything else I should know?"

"Only one thing: after his wife died a couple of years ago, the judge became much more serious. He really loved that woman, so I can understand how her death would change him. Not mean or anything, just, you know, depressed or preoccupied. Sometimes, he appeared as if his mind was somewhere else during some boring testimony or argument. He was still nice, just not as happy, you know what I mean?"

"I can certainly understand how losing a wife like that could change one's view of the world. Thank you, Mr. Simmons. I appreciate your time and answering my questions. You have really helped in our investigation."

"No problem, you take care now."

Luke still had a half an hour before his plane boarded passengers, and there was a line of people seemingly glowering at him to make a seat available in the bar. He tossed off the last of his beer and decided to stretch his legs with a walk around the concourse before he had to endure fitting his six-foot-four frame in an economy seat for two and half hours.

It was a beautiful clear day, and as Luke walked out and back on two long concourses, he saw the snow-capped Olympics to the west and the similarly clad tallest mountains of the Cascades to the east, with Mount Rainier, once again, regally dominating the view to the southeast. This really is lovely country.

Twenty-three

At 7:55 a.m., Luke walked into the Montgomery Street San Francisco office of the Secret Service. Neal Hanson, the special agent in charge, was already in and working on what Luke guessed was his second or third cup of morning coffee.

"Morning, Neal. How're you today?"

"Just fine. How about you? Sounds like Washington was a big success: a murderer, a crooked judge, ten cells of drug dealers up and down the West Coast, and a money-laundering franchise with several outlets. Good work."

"Yeah, it worked out pretty well, but the case that got the whole thing started, the money laundering in that collapsed building in Bellingham, went 'poof' in a cooperation deal."

"But it sounds like it was a good trade—the info he gave up led to all the rest of it and he was just a little cog in a much larger wheel, so net-net, a good deal. By the way, I got a glowing email of commendation about you from an Assistant US Attorney Ennis."

"That's nice. She is a good person, sharp as a tack, and great to work with, as was Sara Donovan, by the way. Neal," Luke paused, "there are still a few pieces of this whole thing from last week that I need to chase down. My typical stuff—tax and bank records—that need to be reviewed to put that whole investigation to bed. I'd be glad to detail what I need to look into if you like."

"No, you take whatever time you need to close out the case. We do have three suspicious activity reports about a guy in San Jose that I will want you to follow up on, but there is no hurry. You can get to them when you wrap up your current case." Neal turned and headed to his office, the only office with actual walls in the whole place, and Luke settled into his cubicle desk, hoping that Mel had been able to forward the requested tax and bank records.

Mel had come through: Luke found the tax returns and bank records for both Parkers in his in-box. He pulled a legal pad from his desk and opened the file. From his days as an undergraduate accounting major at Berkeley and a law student at Hastings, Luke had developed the habit of summarizing financial documents or legal arguments in a combined timeline and flowchart. He had found that patterns can emerge only if the most relevant numbers or important arguments and events are extracted from the avalanche of numbers and dense legal arguments. He started his timeline by writing the years of the records he had before him on a separate page of the legal pad, starting with 2016 and ending with 2020. He opened the 2016 tax filing of Samuel Parker.

2016

– Joint filing with wife, Emma Fay Parker
– Home address listed as a house in Cameron Park (not Granite Bay)
– Only one source of income: Samuel's pay as a public defender
– Deducted maximum amount contributed to an IRA
– Expected home interest deduction

Luke scrolled ahead to bank records and added:

– Saving account $30,000 / average checking balance $5,000

Luke added his own note:

Literally nothing about Samuel Parker's financial life notable, boringly standard, and no apparent effort to fudge on taxes.

He turned the page of his legal pad and similarly reviewed 2017.

2017

— Filed as a single (Divorce?)
— Same address as 2016 (He kept the house
in divorce?)
— No voluntary retirement or charity
contributions (Alimony payments?)
— Savings down to $20,000 and average
checking balance $2,000

Luke continued with 2018.

2018

— Filed as a single
— New address listed as an apartment
in Sacramento
— Cashed out his retirement account and
paid a big hit in taxes and penalties for
early withdrawal
— Savings to zero and checking account to
virtually nothing

Luke stopped his review of documents and went to notes he had taken while he was in Bellingham. The case against Arturo Cruz was dismissed in August of 2018, and Roger Simpson has skipped out on his trial in September of 2018. Luke returned to his chronology and added a note:

> *Samuel Parker sold his house and cashed*
> *out his retirement and savings to get the*
> *startup money for the drug syndicate?*

Luke moved on to 2019.

2019

– Same apartment address as 2018
– Filed using standard deduction, no item-
ized deductions (Tax law changes?)
– No income other than public defender
salary reported

2020

– Filed as a single
– Granite Bay address
– Again, filed with the standard deduction
(No mortgage on new Granite Bay house?)
– Again, no income other than public
defender salary

Luke left his cubicle to get a cup of coffee and was rather pleased with his results so far. Samuel Parker had been a regular guy, but he got divorced, presumably got embittered about his lot in life (maybe exacerbated by alimony), sold his house, and cashed out his retirement and bank accounts to collect sufficient money to get into the drug-trafficking business, about the same time as he recruited Roger Simpson by urging him to skip out on his appearance bond. It all confirmed Mel's explanation.

Luke returned to his cubicle and started on the same procedure for the senior Parker.

2016

– *Joint return with wife, Carol*
– *Address Point Loma Circle*
– *Only income reported was judicial salary*
– *No home interest deduction (Owned home free and clear?)*
– *Maximized voluntary retirement contributions*
– *Savings account balance of around $90 K and average checking balance $10 K*
– *Plain Jane return; no apparent effort the fudge on taxes*

2017

– *Joint return*
– *No voluntary retirement contributions*
– *High medical deductions, resulted in lower taxes than last year*

2018

– *Filed jointly, same address*
– *Large home interest deduction (Refinanced house?)*
– *No voluntary retirement contributions.*
– *Cashed out retirement account, which increased tax liability considerably*
– *Large medical expenses*
– *Only income reported from judgeship*

— Savings down to $10 K, checking account balances often near zero
— (Same pattern as Samuel Parker: took out a huge loan on house and cashed out retirement and savings accounts to fund their startup costs? Together, how much had they been able to gather up to start their business?)

2019

— Joint filing
— Same address
— Very high medical expenses
— No retirement contributions
— High home interest deduction
— Savings down to $5 K

2020

— Joint filing
— No home interest deductions (Paid off mortgage taken out in 2018?)
— Extremely high medical deduction.

Luke leaned back in his chair and rubbed his eyes. It was clear that, indeed, Mel had been right. Father and son decided together to go into the drug trade, they got their hands on as much cash as they could—selling Samuel's home and mortgaging the father's home, cashing in retirement accounts, emptying saving accounts—and went into business. When the money started rolling in, the son bought himself a mansion in Granite Bay and the judge paid off the mortgage he had taken out. Neither needed to bother with additional saving for retirement, as they were flush with enough cash to last them the rest of their lives—a successful business startup. What they did not count on, apparently, was the danger of employing people like Arturo Cruz to manage their enterprise. Stupid. Stupid. Stupid.

Just as Luke was about to close the computer files and ask his boss about the details of the next "suspicious activity" investigation, he slapped his forehead. "What the hell?" he said to himself. "I should have seen it earlier. I thought the judge was a widower." He settled his chair back in front of the computer and searched the online record of death certificates in California for a record of the death of Carol Parker. A lot of Carol Parkers had died, so he went back into the tax returns and found that the full name was Carol Jean Parker and entered the full name in the computer search of death certificates. No Carol Jean Parker.

Luke had only examined the part of the tax returns that were the 1040s, the two-page summaries, not the 1040 As, detailing the specifics of the itemized deductions. He discovered that the medical expenses that the judge had deducted had been paid to a variety of clinics, hospitals, and doctors in the San Diego area for 2017 and 2018, but that 2018 also reported ever-increasing bills from a clinic in Saranac, New York. All the medical bills for 2019 and 2020 had been from the same clinic in New York, the Smithfield Clinic.

Luke did not know if New York had a searchable file for death certificates, like California, but hoped they did. Many states had not yet joined the twenty-first century and collected and digitized their records. Only a few keystrokes later, Luke found that a death certificate had been filed for a Carol Jean Parker in Saranac, New York. She had died on February 21, 2021, just five months ago. The listed cause of death was complications of Siddell's Syndrome.

Luke looked at his watch and calculated that it was 2:45 in the afternoon in New York. He looked up the website of the Smithfield Clinic and dialed the listed phone number.

"Hello, Smithfield Clinic. How may I help you?"

"Hello, my name is Lucas Bitterman, an investigator from the San Francisco field office of the Secret Service, and I would like to speak to whoever is in charge."

"The Secret Service? Is the President sick or something?"

"No, ma'am. I just need to speak with the director, or chief executive, or whoever is in charge."

"Okay, I'll connect you with Dr. Dipak Krishnamurthi; he is our medical director and the owner of Smithfield Clinic."

After what seemed to Luke to be an inordinately rude wait, a voice came on the line, "Hello, I am Dr. Krishnamurthi. I understand you are with the Secret Service and wish to speak with me."

"Yes, Dr. Krishnamurthi. I am Lucas Bitterman, from the San Francisco office, and I have some questions I hope you can help me with."

"I'll do what I can, Mr. Bitterman. What are your questions?"

"I understand that Mrs. Carol Jean Parker was a patient of yours. Is that correct?"

"Mr. Bitterman, I am sure you are aware that under the HIPAA requirements, I am not allowed to discuss the details of any patient or even confirm that any individual even is a patient. I am sorry I cannot help you."

"Dr. Krishnamurthi, I appreciate your adherence to the HIPAA requirements, but I am sure you are aware that healthcare providers have an exemption from HIPAA disclosure limitations in response to inquiries from law enforcement. I am also aware, from public records, that Mrs. Parker died about five months ago from complications of Siddell's Syndrome. All I want is some general information about that condition and the costs of treating patients with that condition. Your clinic is not in any trouble here; I just need some information. We can tap dance and go through subpoenaing information and tie you up for the next month or two with lawyers, or we can have a conversation now and you'll not hear from me again."

After a long silence, Dr. Krishnamurthi softly asked, "What is it you wish to know, Mr. Bitterman?"

"Thank you. First, what is Siddell's Syndrome?"

"Siddell's Syndrome is actually the combination of two exceedingly rare conditions. The first is a neuromuscular degenerative disease that atrophies the muscles and causes excruciating pain in the muscles and joints. The second is a condition that causes fat to accumulate in the extremities: the arms, feet, and legs. Each is extremely rare, fewer than two hundred cases a year worldwide, but in about eighty percent of the cases, patients suffer from both conditions—thus Siddell's Syndrome, named after the British physician who first described it in the medical literature."

"What is the prognosis of people diagnosed with Siddell's Syndrome?"

"It is not good. Few live more than a few months after diagnosis. The truly insidious part of this syndrome is that the two conditions that cause such extreme pain and disfiguring accumulations of fat do not typically affect the brain, so patients are totally aware of what is happening to them. In most cases, as the patients deteriorate, they are put into a medically induced coma and allowed to die."

"But Mrs. Parker was being treated?"

"Yes. We specialize in medical treatment for people suffering from rare and incurable diseases. In this case, there are a couple of drug interventions that do not cure the disease but can arrest the progression of the symptoms."

"I assume that such treatment is expensive."

"Criminally so. The drugs alone for the two conditions run between seventy-five thousand dollars and one hundred thousand dollars a month. As I said, they do not cure the disease; they simply allow the patient to live, totally cognizant of what is going on. In addition, these patients need twenty-four-hour monitoring because the dosing of these drugs is day-to-day and depends on patient response. Such residential medical attention is also quite expensive."

"So, this is the treatment regimen that was offered to Mrs. Parker?'

"Yes, and her husband and son knew that this treatment would likely only delay the inevitable. From the time of her admission, both visited at least once a month but only stayed a day and half or so. They spent their whole time here with Mrs. Parker."

"How did the Parkers pay for it? I mean, that's a lot of money."

"Mr. Bitterman, I don't know. I negotiated with the two drug companies involved and got a modest reduction in the price of the treatments, but the total bill still came in just under one hundred and seventy-five thousand dollars a month."

"Were they current with your charges when Mrs. Parker passed away?"

"Yes," he paused, "but it was obviously a struggle for them. At the beginning, the elder Parker wrote personal checks and stayed current, then there were a few months when they started falling behind, and then we started getting checks drawn on a foreign bank and they caught up and stayed current."

"You say a foreign bank? Do recall which bank?"

"Yes, I was apprehensive because it was a Panamanian bank. I think it was called the Pan American Guaranty

Bank, and the checks took quite a while to clear, but they always did."

"Dr. Krishnamurthi, I thank you for the information."

"You're most welcome, Mr. Bitterman, and I hope that Mr. Parker and his son are okay. They are both genuinely nice gentlemen and cared deeply for Mrs. Parker."

"Dr. Krishnamurthi, thank you."

"Thank you."

Luke was almost sick at the sadness of what he had uncovered. Samuel and Harold Parker were not simply drug-dealing and money-laundering creeps, they were caught up in a system where the price of drugs and treatment for their beloved wife and mother all but forced them into the drug trade. They did not have any extended family and a limited social network, so a GoFundMe appeal would probably have been futile, certainly for the amounts involved. They did not have any assets other than their retirement accounts and homes, which they liquidated or mortgaged to the hilt. When the drug money started to come in, they collected proceeds in Bitcoin, transferred it on to a Panamanian bank, and were able to keep up with Mrs. Parker's medical expenses, pay off the senior Parker's mortgage, and buy a new house for the younger Parker. It appears likely that the younger Parker had sole control over the Panamanian account, and with him now deceased, the millions likely there will languish until the bank seizes the balance of an inactive account.

With another half hour online, Luke learned that the purchase of the son's house in Granite Bay and the retirement of the mortgage on the senior Parker's house were both accomplished with checks from the Pan American Guaranty Bank, Panama City.

Luke answered an incoming call on his cell phone. "Mr. Bitterman, this is Dr. Krishnamurthi. I am afraid I might not have been as forthcoming as I should have been when we talked a little while ago."

"Okay, what might you have left out?"

"Well, I should have told you that after the death of Mrs. Parker, the checks from that Panamanian bank kept on coming, only for much larger amounts. You see, when Harold and Samuel came here to make arrangements after Mrs. Parker died, they asked about our foundation. We are organized as a non-profit clinic and have a foundation set up to solicit and receive donations in support of our work. Within a few weeks, we started receiving rather large checks anonymously donated to our foundation but drawn from the same Panamanian bank."

"How large were the checks?"

"Oh my, they were large: four to six hundred thousand dollars a month."

"You say they were anonymous. They didn't identify any donor or particular patient account?"

"No, they were made out to the foundation with the notation of 'donation to the foundation.' I hope we aren't in any trouble for accepting these donations."

"I would recommend that you consult with your own attorney, but I don't think there is a problem here. Is that all you needed to update me about?"

"Ah, yes. For the last five months, I naturally assumed the Parkers were behind the donations. They are awfully nice people, and they both loved Mrs. Parker very much."

"All right then. Thanks, Dr. Krishnamurthi."

Luke looked at the clock on the wall and had not realized how quickly his day had gotten away from him; he had his annual physical appointment in just twenty minutes. He grabbed his coat, stopped by Neal's office, and told him he had to scoot to make his doctor appointment.

"You can't miss that, Luke. Now that things are opening again, I imagine if you missed that appointment, you wouldn't get another for months. See you tomorrow."

Twenty-four

Luke was surprised to find that Annie and Ashley were not home when he walked into their Marina District house. He found a note in the middle of the kitchen table that explained their absence: "Out for a run with Ashley in her stroller. Home around 5:30ish."

Luke smiled as he figured his wife must be planning on a good long run. Ashley loved going fast in the stroller, and Annie was fully back to her pre-pregnancy physical conditioning. Luke went upstairs and changed out his "school clothes," as his mother had taught him to do, and returned to the kitchen to make a pot of coffee.

Annie parked the stroller, picked up Ashley, and joined her husband in the kitchen. "So, how was your physical? I'll bet the doc told you that you needed to get more exercise."

"Actually, Dr. Perlman told me I was as healthy as a pudgy horse and only prescribed that I at least try to keep up with you."

"Fat chance, pun intended."

"Speaking of healthy, how about I order a pizza for us for dinner?"

"I know I have burned off enough calories to have a couple of slices, but I worry that pizza might just get in the way of your belt. How about Chinese?"

"Deal." Luke picked up his phone and ordered their usual Chinese meal. "It will be here in about thirty minutes. So how was your run?"

"The best since Ashley arrived on the scene. We did the four-mile loop down to Marina Green and up through the Park and back, and to my absolute delight, I could have done another mile or two. Maybe this weekend, we can do a hike up Mount Tamalpais."

"With me carrying Ashley in the backpack, of course."

"Of course."

"If I am doing the carrying, I reserve the right to choose the short trail, rather than the seven-mile backbreaker."

"Okay, but we might have to do it twice, depending on how much you eat tonight."

"While we are waiting for dinner, hon, I have a situation at work that I really think you might be able to help me with."

"Sure, what's going on in the life of Special Agent Lucas Bitterman?"

Luke spent the next twenty minutes relating the details of his trip to Bellingham: the earthquake, the collapsed building, the discovered money and computers, the identification of Cruz and his amazing drug delivery trip up the West Coast, his capture on I-5, the murder of the young Parker, and the corruption of Judge Parker.

"But here's the problem, love. I have subsequently learned that the Parkers started their drug syndicate simply to pay exorbitant medical costs for their gravely ill wife and mother. She had a rare condition that cost around one hundred and fifty or two hundred thousand dollars a month. Both Parkers appear to have been stand-up guys before Mrs. Parker got sick. The judge's bailiff says that in his five or six years in the judge's court, the only hinky trial was that of Arturo Cruz; every other case was handled appropriately. He wasn't a hanging judge or a bleeding heart, just a straight-down-the-line judge. Nothing spectacular or unusual. Now here is the weird part. After Mrs. Parker died, they appear to have donated a lot of the monthly drug-trafficking proceeds to the clinic where Mrs. Parker was treated."

"You're making them sound like Robin Hoods, sympathetic characters who robbed from the rich and gave to the poor. They did start and run a drug syndicate and feed that crap to addicts up and down the West Coast. And the son got murdered in the process."

Luke realized he had framed the issue in a way that Annie would react in this fashion. Too many of the children she treated were traumatized from birth by living in drug-dominated households. "Actually, rather than Robin Hood, I was thinking about Iran–Contra."

"I've heard of that, but what was it?"

"The analogy just occurred to me as I was thinking about this case, though I had forgotten the details. So, I looked it up. In the Reagan administration, people facilitated the sale of arms to Iran, contrary to US policy, in order to get the money to fund the Nicaraguan rebels, also contrary to US policy. In short, they engaged in crime in order to support what they believed was a good, though illegal, cause."

"You know, I don't care if what they did was Robin Hood or Iran–Contra, they still operated an illegal drug-trafficking operation and the judge criminally released an actual drug trafficker to help him."

"Would you be more forgiving if they had embezzled money from a condo association to pay for the mother's medical bills?"

Annie paused before answering, "Yes, yes, I would. What does the judge have to say about this whole mess?"

"As far as I know, he hasn't said one word since his arrest. He hasn't even asked for an attorney. I suspect the guy is totally devastated. His wife is dead, his son is murdered, and he is going to lose his life's work on the bench and his pension. He has lost everything. I think it safe to assume that he is never going to start and run a drug syndicate again."

"Going back to the beginning. Didn't the judge have health insurance that would have paid those huge bills?"

"He did, and I don't know why so much of the burden fell directly on him, but I suspect that, as the disease was extremely rare, every treatment effort would be regarded as experimental and not be covered and that the drugs required were not included in the prescription formulary in the insurance plan. In short, he might have a plan that covered illnesses, just not rare and expensive ones."

"So, you think that the father should get to walk away from this?"

"Actually, yes, I do."

"Luke, that's why I love you so much. I think you are probably right, and justice would be properly served by looking the other way after all the sleaziest elements of this episode are prosecuted and put in jail. My only question is can the system do that? Look the other way on the judge and prosecute all the sleaze-balls lower on the food chain?"

"I don't know, but tomorrow I am going to find out. You know, the really complicating part of this is that if the judge is convicted of corruption, I suspect hundreds of lawyers will file briefs for convicted clients to get a new trial or be released because their judge was corrupt. In short, the US attorney down there in San Diego might just cut him loose, not because he was financially unable to fund his wife's treatment any other way, but because it will cause a raft of time-consuming and difficult days in court."

The doorbell rang and Luke gathered in their Chinese dinner.

After dinner, Annie announced that she was going to give Ashley a bath in the bathtub. "I know she has enjoyed her baths in the kitchen sink, but she is getting too big. I will sit next to the tub and see how she does. I'll bet you she loves it."

"I am sure she will. You know, we probably should ditch all those pictures we have taken of her naked in the kitchen sink. I am sure when she is thirteen or fourteen, those pictures would embarrass the hell out of her."

"Don't I know it! My mom had dozens of those kinds of pictures of me, and as you said, when I was a teenager, I threw a hissy-fit and demanded that she destroy them. She didn't, but she did take them out of my baby book and hid them away. You will never see them."

"You go ahead. I am going to give Mom a call."

Annie took Ashley upstairs for her inaugural bathtub bath while Luke called his mom.

"Hi, Mom, do you have a minute to chat?"

Liz was puzzled by Luke's serious tone. "Always, Luke."

"I know you have never talked about it, but I imagine in your years of medical practice, you had several occasions when the best course of action for a patient was not clear, but a decision had to be made."

"Of course, hon, that's the hardest part of being a physician. Why do you ask?"

"Mom, I think there might be a parallel between what I do as a law enforcement officer and your experience as a physician."

"Well, there obviously is. Both are professions, and professions always involve judgements most average folks don't want to have to make or bear the burden of being wrong in their decisions."

"That's exactly what I am talking about. How did you make these kinds of decisions?"

"Fortunately, I didn't have to make such decisions very often, unlike continuing-care physicians, like oncologists, cardiologists, or neurologists do. But I can tell you that there is no easy shortcut; each case is different, and you never can be certain that your decision is right. A lot of doctors simply can't deal with it and either move into less stressful medical careers or give up completely."

Luke chuckled. "You might remember, Mom, that that was precisely my frustration in law school and on the bar exam—it seemed like the best legal answer always was 'it depends.'"

"They don't distribute a chart in medical school that says, 'If *a*, do *x*' or 'If *b*, do *y*.' They are always harder decisions than that."

"Well, Mom, I can tell you that some decisions we have to make in the criminal justice system have to be made without any guidance other than one's own personal sense of what is right, and it sucks. Fortunately, I am in the law enforcement part of the system and it is not directly my call to make decisions about justice—that's up to prosecutors, juries, and judges—but I still know that information coming out of our investigations could, or should, be part of the administration or justice, and it often isn't."

"Luke, I wouldn't trust anyone to make those kinds of decisions more than you. You are a smart, caring, and decent person and understand the consequences of decisions made in the system. There is nothing more you can do other than try to make them wisely."

"I was afraid that would be your answer. I was hoping that maybe there was a guidebook or a set of principles that could take the weight off my shoulders, but I know that hope was silly. I get it. I guess that is why we get the big bucks. Sorry to intrude on your evening in this way."

"No intrusion at all, Luke. I am delighted you thought I might be of some assistance."

"Oh, you were, but it still doesn't make it any easier. Maybe I should have become an accountant, after all."

"No, Luke, you would have been so bored so quickly that we would all fear you might run off and join the circus."

"Well, Annie is the one attending the circus right now. She is giving Ashley her first bath in the bathtub. I think I better go up and check on them."

"You do that and take some pictures of Ashley in the tub for me."

"Love ya, Mom." Luke hung up and smiled. It seemed Ashley would simply have to put up with pictures of her in the sink and the bathtub.

Twenty-five

The next morning, Luke explained to Neal what he had uncovered about the origins of the Parker drug syndicate, and together they phoned Assistant US Attorney Melody Ennis. Luke, once again, reiterated the results of his investigation. When the call ended, Neal congratulated Luke and reminded him that there were some reports of suspicious financial activity that needed to be investigated.

"Remember, Luke, investigate, arrest, investigate some more, testify, repeat."

"Got it, Neal. I'm about to start repeating."

***

Five weeks after Luke had finished his part of the Parker investigation, he got a text from Mel: "I thought you would like to know that in exchange for telling us everything he knew about the drug trafficking, which, frankly, wasn't much, charges against the judge were dropped and he was allowed to retire, with his pension intact."

Luke reflected on the difference between simply catching bad guys and being part of a system that sought justice. Was the law enforced in this case? Was justice served? He wished he knew.

Author's Notes and Acknowledgements

I would like to apologize to my family and friends in Bellingham—and probably to the Chamber of Commerce—for raising the often-forgotten existence of coal mine tunnels under Bellingham and environs. They do exist, hundreds of miles of them. Over the years, some of them have, in fact, caused subsidence problems for buildings and streets. At this point, however, they are likely only noteworthy as an introduction in a novel. Fortunately, there are several resources available for anyone interested in learning more about the history and operation of the coal mines of Whatcom County, including several videos and publications from the Whatcom County Historical Society and a variety of US Geological Survey reports. I hope my characterization of Bellingham and the Northwest as a charming and interesting place to live or visit makes up for any angst my recalling the existence of the mine tunnels may have caused.

All writers work with the same million words in the English language; actually, most only work with the 170,000 words currently in use or the 30,000 or so words of the average person's lexicon. Nevertheless, some phrases are so enchanting or characteristic of a particular author that their use by other writers must be acknowledged; such is the case of the moniker "byte witch," used to describe DEA Agent Donovan's uncanny computer skills. I first heard and always remembered that expression from Tom Clancy, the author of dozens of techno-thriller and spy stories. Many years ago, when I was dean of a college, my office needed a short-term technical consultant to help with some computer-networking issues. A young woman applied who had all the requisite skills and experience and who listed Tom Clancy as one of her references. She included his phone number, so I decided to check out the reference and phoned the number listed, fully expecting to reach an agent's or publisher's office. A nice woman answered the call, and when I asked to speak to Tom Clancy, she called out, "Tom, phone's for you." Then, "Tom Clancy here." I explained my need for a technical consultant and that I was checking references for Ms. Jones (not her real name). "Oh, she's a real byte witch!" As a fan of his books, I knew immediately and conclusively that I was, in fact, speaking to *the* Tom Clancy. We had a delightful chat. I hoped that one day I would have the opportunity to appropriately use the expression and to gratefully acknowledge its origin. The reading world misses the voice of Jack Ryan and numerous other stories well told.

I acknowledge that I depicted a simplified version of the cryptocurrency world. There are plenty of technically dense or practically useful guides to navigating alternative currencies. It is accurate, however, that the universe of cryptocurrencies cries out for regularization: consumer protection, adequate reporting requirements, reasonable accountability measures, and regulation. Of course, the absence of reporting, accountability, and regulation is precisely the reason so many cryptocurrency advocates are drawn to that world in the first place, so edging in that direction will be difficult.

I want to acknowledge and thank several people who read early drafts of this novel: Leatha King, Eugene Fairbanks, Carol Barbo, and Marva Knox. Each read drafts and offered invaluable comments and suggestions on the story development, characters, writing, dialogue—indeed, every element in the evolution of a novel. The book, and I, are the better for their assistance and I appreciate each of them greatly. Of course, remaining errors or flaws are all mine.

I particularly appreciate the permission of Eugene S. Fairbanks for the use of his poem, "Northwest Rivers." An abridged version of this poem was the winner of the 2020 Sue C. Boynton Poetry Contest.

Finally, I did, indeed, climb Mount Rainier, about forty pounds and forty years ago.

Stephen W. King
Chico, California

Stephen W. King is an author and retired university dean. During his academic career, he published several college textbooks and numerous research papers. In retirement, he turned to writing fiction, publishing All That Glisters Is Not Gold in 2020, introducing readers to Lucas Bitterman. Follow the Crypto grew out of Stephen's interest in the evolving cryptocurrency phenomenon. Readers are once again invited to explore both technical and ethical issues of law enforcement and the administration of justice with Luke as their guide.

Stephen lives with his wife of fifty-four years in Chico, California.

Follow Luke and me on Twitter @StephenWKing1
and at www.swkingbooks.com.
Contact me at steve@swkingbooks.com.